Dear Reader,

It often seems that people lucky enough to have close families take them for granted. And yet, the lack of family can leave scars that never seem to fade. My heroine, Emily McBride, has more scars than most.

Ever since she was a little girl, Emily had longed for a real family. Her father was cold and distant, her mother long missing, and her beloved older brother had left town years ago. Now she's all alone and planning to escape from the hometown that has begun to seem like a cage. She's poised on the brink of a new life—and then Wade Davenport comes to town with his adorable eight-year-old son....

I've thoroughly enjoyed getting to know Savannah, Tara and Emily McBride, and I'm lucky enough to be able to give them the happy ending each woman deserves. But there is still one McBride whose story has not been told. Lucas McBride, the true black sheep of the family, left Honoria under a cloud of suspicion and has been alone ever since. Being the matchmaker I am, I can't simply *leave* him that way! So Lucas is coming back to Honoria, just in time for Christmas, to face the younger sister he abandoned, the townspeople who suspect him of murder...and to finally find the answers to the questions that have been haunting him.

I hope you enjoy *Enticing Emily.* And be sure to watch for Lucas's story in December 1998. And now, back to those scandalous McBrides....

Enjoy,

Gina Wilkins

Gina Wilkins
ENTICING EMILY

Harlequin Books

TORONTO • NEW YORK • LONDON
AMSTERDAM • PARIS • SYDNEY • HAMBURG
STOCKHOLM • ATHENS • TOKYO • MILAN
MADRID • WARSAW • BUDAPEST • AUCKLAND

For my guys—
John, who takes me to all the classiest places.
And David, who loves *Star Wars* and stuffed tigers.
I love you both.

ISBN 0-373-25784-8

ENTICING EMILY

Prologue

OF THE THREE McBride cousins, twenty-six-year-old Emily was the only one who appeared to be enjoying their afternoon outing in the woods behind her house. Which might have seemed odd to some, considering that Emily had seen her father buried only hours earlier.

It wasn't that Emily was hard-hearted. But her father had been ill for a very long time, suffering in a way that made his death almost a relief. For five long years Emily had cared for him, nursed him, tried to comfort him. She needed this time for herself, even if it was only for a visit with Savannah and Tara in the Georgia woods where they'd spent so many pleasant hours as children.

Fifteen years ago, as a lark to fill a lazy summer afternoon, the cousins had buried an old cypress chest containing individual plastic boxes filled with mementos of their childhood. A time capsule, they'd called it. They'd made a solemn vow to dig it up on Savannah's thirtieth birthday. Though that occasion was still a few weeks away, Emily had talked the other two into unearthing it today, since they were all together.

"I'm not sure this is such a good idea," Savannah had protested, looking strangely reluctant.

"It has only been fifteen years," Tara agreed. "Time-capsule contents are much more interesting after more time has passed, don't you think?"

Emily firmly shook her head. "We've already trekked out here and dug it up. And we're only a few weeks away from Savannah's birthday, the date we originally agreed upon. We might as well open it."

For some reason, this was something Emily really wanted to do. Maybe she simply wanted to be reminded of happier times.

Emily suspected that Savannah finally went along out of sympathy for her. Perhaps Savannah had suddenly decided that Emily needed a diversion from the sorrow of the past few days. But Savannah probably had no idea how badly Emily needed to be distracted from fretting about the future.

Digging into the garbage bags, encrusted with dried mud that had protected the objects within the chest, Savannah extracted the three shoebox-sized plastic boxes. Each one had a name written on the top in permanent marker. Emily accepted hers with an eagerness that was notably lacking in her cousins.

She didn't know why they were so reluctant to indulge in a bit of nostalgia. Emily had very happy memories of the day they'd buried these boxes. She'd thought the whole thing a marvelous adventure, and she'd been thrilled that her cousins had included her. She'd idolized Savannah and Tara, who'd been fifteen and almost fourteen at the time, compared to Emily's mere eleven. They'd been surprisingly patient with her, never seeming to mind when she tagged along on their afternoons spent giggling and gossiping in this clearing in the woods.

Emily couldn't help smiling as she pulled one item

after another out of her box. A plastic clown figurine she'd won at the county fair. A perfect-attendance ribbon from school. A necklace she'd made with lacquered pasta shells. A Barbie dress...now why had she thought that would be significant fifteen years later?

Her smile faded when she discovered a photograph of her family—herself as a baby, surrounded by her father, her mother and her half brother Lucas. Emily was the only one in the photograph who looked happy to be there.

And then she found the letter she'd written to herself. Scanning the childish handwriting, she winced as she read her grandiose plans of seeing the world outside the limits of tiny Honoria, Georgia. She'd pictured a future life filled with family—her father and brother, her aunts, uncles, cousins, a husband and children.

She had never imagined being so alone in this town that had once felt like home.

She was just about to close the box when she felt something wrapped in tissue paper at the bottom. She didn't remember putting anything else in, but it had been a long time. Mildly curious, she fumbled in the wrapping and pulled out something heavy and solid.

It was a bracelet. Gold. Fashioned of heavy, carved links, with an ornate, solid oval clasp. It looked very old—antique, maybe.

Emily didn't remember ever seeing this bracelet in her life.

And then she frowned and looked again at that old family photograph. Her gaze focused on her mother, Nadine Peck McBride. Specifically, she studied Nadine's right arm, which was wrapped protectively around the baby in her lap.

Emily's eyes widened, and her fingers clenched convulsively around the piece of jewelry.

Her mother had been missing for a long time. How had Nadine's bracelet gotten into this box when Emily knew for certain that *she* hadn't put it there?

1

"So I SAID to Arthur, 'Why don't we ask Emily? I'm sure she would be happy to help us out.' And Arthur said, 'Of course. Ask Emily.'" Martha Godwin rattled the ice in her tea glass and smiled in sheer delight at her own cleverness.

Ask Emily. It seemed to be the unofficial motto of Honoria, Georgia, the little town in which Emily Mc-Bride had been born and raised. The town she'd rarely left in her entire twenty-six years.

Need a baby-sitter? Ask Emily.

Someone to pick up your mail and newspaper while you're on vacation? Ask Emily.

A ride to the doctor's office or the grocery store? Ask Emily.

Need a dress hemmed? A few dozen cookies for a bake sale? Someone to go door-to-door collecting charity donations? Someone to substitute in the three-year-olds' Sunday-school class? Just ask Emily.

With her fixed smile masking her rebellious thoughts—or so she hoped—Emily answered genially. "Of course, Martha. I'd be happy to take care of Oliver while you and Arthur are away on your cruise."

Martha nodded in satisfaction. "I knew you'd help us out. You're such a sweet girl, Emily. I don't know what we'd do without you around here."

Well, you're going to find out, Emily thought. *Three more months, and I'm leaving. Then you and the rest of Honoria will have to find someone else to do your "little favors."*

But all she said was, "When did you say you're leaving?"

"Monday. And, gracious, I have so much to do in only three short days! You have no idea how much packing is involved for a week-long cruise."

Of course she didn't. Emily had never taken a cruise. She'd never flown on an airplane or ridden a train or traveled outside the borders of her own country. But that was all going to change.

Five months ago, Emily had buried her father, the last tie holding her to this town. And she'd given herself until the end of the year to settle his affairs. Then, finally, she was going to find a life for herself. Somewhere other than Honoria, preferably. She was going to find out once and for all who she was and what she wanted out of life. She was going to see all those places she'd only read about in books during those long nights sitting by her father's sickbed.

"Why don't you bring Oliver over Sunday afternoon so you won't have that to do Monday morning?" she suggested to the older woman, putting her lofty future plans aside for the moment.

Martha patted her mouth with a paper napkin. "Would you mind too terribly coming to our house Sunday afternoon to pick him up? I'm afraid Arthur and I will be so very busy Sunday that we really won't have time to drive all the way out here in the country."

Oh, now that was just too much. Not only did the Godwins want her to take care of their geriatric poodle for a week, they wanted her to come *get* the little mutt. And Martha didn't even seem to have an inkling of how presumptuous she was being.

"All right," was all Emily said. "What time should I come by?"

You're such a doormat, Emily McBride. But that, too, was going to stop when she finally took off on her own, she promised herself.

"Anytime between one and three will be fine. Oh, dear, look at the time. I really must go. I want to stop by the police station on my way home."

"The police station?" Emily repeated curiously.

Martha nodded her carefully frosted head. "I want to remind Chief Davenport that I'll be out of town next week. I've asked him to send extra patrols around our place several times a night, but I'm afraid he'll forget. To be honest, Emily, there are times when I wonder if our new chief of police is very bright."

"I haven't met him," Emily admitted, "but I read in the Honoria *Gazette* that he came highly recommended from his last position. I understand he was the mayor's first choice after Chief Powell resigned."

"That may be, but I certainly haven't been very impressed so far. In the short time he's been here, I've never seen him move any faster than a stroll, nor does he seem capable of standing without leaning against something. Arthur says you could set the man's hair afire and it would take him an hour to get around to putting it out."

Emily chuckled. "Still, he must be good at his job or Mayor McQuade would never have appointed him."

"I suppose you're right." Martha smiled. "It isn't as if there's ever any real crime in Honoria. Teenagers getting out of hand, Joe Wimble getting drunk and making noise every Saturday night, the occasional petty theft. There hasn't been a serious crime here since...since..."

Since Roger Jennings was murdered fifteen years ago. Martha didn't have to finish the sentence. Emily knew exactly what crime the other woman had been about to mention. After all, it had been Emily's brother who'd unfairly taken the blame for it.

Martha didn't stay much longer. She'd gotten what she wanted, and was in a hurry to be off so she could impose on others.

Emily closed the door behind her visitor, sighed, and ran a hand through her blond curls. She turned away from the door and spotted the corner of a glossy, brightly colored travel brochure sticking out from beneath a stack of bills on the antique desk. She smiled.

Three more months, and she would be free. The idea was as exhilarating as it was terrifying.

"EMILY, ARE YOU absolutely sure you want to do this?" Mary Kay Evans asked solemnly, extending a pen in Emily's direction.

Emily took the pen firmly in her hand and carefully signed her name at the bottom of the contract in front of her. Only then did she look up at the woman across the desk. "I'm sure, Mary Kay. This is something I've been planning for a very long time."

"But your home...you've lived there all your life. It's all you have left of your family. You really want to sell it?"

Emily's smile felt strained. "Mary Kay, why are you suddenly trying to talk me out of this? You've already told me you expect to get a nice commission from selling my place. Do you want the listing or not?"

"I want it. If, that is, you're absolutely certain you're doing the right thing."

Trying to look as confident as she sounded, Emily replied, "I'm absolutely certain. A four-bedroom house on twenty acres of land is more than I need. And there's nothing holding me here now that Dad's gone, so I'll have a chance to do some traveling. Do you really blame me?"

"I guess not," Mary Kay replied. She had spent four years at a college in the east before returning to Honoria to marry her high-school sweetheart. "It's just that...well, I never thought you would leave," she admitted. "I know all your cousins have moved away, but I thought your roots were deeper. I thought you would always stay in Honoria."

Had Mary Kay honestly believed that Emily would be content to live the rest of her life alone in the house that every member of her dysfunctional family had abandoned one by one—either by choice or, in her father's case, by death? Maybe the other woman thought Emily would marry eventually. But even if Emily hadn't been so restless and ready to leave, the prospects in Honoria were decidedly limited.

Emily reached for her purse. "It's not as if I'll never come back to visit. My aunt and uncle still live here, and always will, I suppose. And I'll want to see all my old friends again. But this is what I want to do now. What I *need* to do."

Mary Kay nodded briskly. "In that case," she said, stacking the paperwork neatly in front of her, "you've come to the right place. As a matter of fact, I have someone in mind already who just might be interested in your house."

Emily felt a sudden hollowness somewhere deep inside her. "Already?" she asked in surprise.

"Yes. He came in yesterday and I mentioned that I might have a place coming available today. He's a widower with a young son, and your house is very much like what he's looking for. I wouldn't be surprised if he makes an offer as soon as he sees it."

"Oh." Emily moistened her lips, which suddenly felt dry. "Well, that would be...great," she said rather lamely.

"Maybe you know him. He's the new— Oh, here he is now."

Hearing the door to the real-estate office open behind her, Emily turned. The man who strolled in was not overly tall, maybe five foot ten. Through his chambray shirt and close-fitting jeans, she could tell that he was solidly built, with strong arms, broad shoulders and lean hips. He walked with the confidence of a man who was accustomed to being in charge. His hair was brown, shot with red, conservatively cut, a bit disheveled by the autumn breeze. His eyes were brown. Rich, warm brown, but sharp enough that Emily suspected there was very little he missed.

She wouldn't have called him classically handsome, but that didn't seem to matter. He had an attraction all his own, and Emily imagined that most women would agree with her.

"Hello, Chief Davenport. I was just talking about you," Mary Kay said with a flirtatiousness that confirmed Emily's theory. Mary Kay was happily married, but obviously not immune to a good-looking man.

"Were you?" The man smiled, pushing lazy dimples into his tanned cheeks, and looked curiously at Emily.

Mary Kay made the introductions. "Emily McBride, this is Wade Davenport, Honoria's new police chief. Chief Davenport, Emily owns the house I mentioned to you yesterday. The four-bedroom frame with the wraparound porch and twenty acres of land?"

"Nice to meet you, Ms. McBride," Wade Davenport said in a drawl that made it clear that he might be new to Honoria, but was as Southern as any other resident of his new hometown.

Emily placed her hand in his, trying to reconcile the man in front of her with Martha Godwin's description of the new police chief. Martha had implied that Wade Davenport was a bit slow. Emily didn't believe that for a moment.

She remembered that Mary Kay had mentioned that he was widowed and a single father. How sad that he'd lost his wife so young, she thought with a tug of sympathy.

"Ms. Evans was telling me about your house yesterday," he said. "Since I've moved here, I've been looking for a place with a big yard and lots of room for my son to run in, and yours sounds ideal. But Ms. Evans wasn't sure you were committed to selling it?"

"Oh, but I am," Emily replied decisively. "I've just signed the papers. My father passed away a few months ago, and the house is just too big for me now."

"I've noticed several new apartment complexes being built in town. Seems like quite a few others around here have decided not to bother with maintenance and yard work," he commented, not quite prying.

"Actually, I'll be leaving Honoria," she replied.

"I'm sorry to hear that," he murmured.

That was when she realized that he was still holding her hand. And looking at her in a way that made her pulse jump.

She quickly pulled her hand away. "Mary Kay will tell you about the house," she said, keeping her voice brusque as she tucked her purse beneath her arm. "If you're interested, she'll set up an appointment for you to see it. It was very nice to meet you, Chief Davenport, but I really have to go now."

With a quick nod at Mary Kay, she made her exit from the real-estate office. She was aware that she'd been a bit abrupt, but she'd had a sudden need to get away. She felt as if she'd just burned her bridges, and the smell of imaginary smoke was suddenly beginning to choke her.

"I'M TELLING YOU, Davenport, someone's been stealing money out of my business account," Dr. Sam Jennings, the town dentist, stated loudly. "And I'm pretty damn sure who. It's that McBride woman."

Marshall Hayes, president of First Bank of Honoria, frowned and wrung his hands. "Now, Sam, calm down. You can't go throwing accusations like that around without evidence. Can he, Chief Davenport?"

Leaning one shoulder against a wall in the bank president's office, Wade Davenport rubbed his chin for a moment before answering. "It's always best to have reasonable proof before naming names," he agreed. "Do you have evidence to support your accusation, Dr. Jennings?"

"She's a McBride," the angry man answered with a scowl. "That's all the evidence I need."

"That's hardly fair." Marshall Hayes was obviously annoyed, but still careful not to alienate one of his bank's more profitable clients. "Emily is a fine young woman. She's never caused a bit of trouble in this town, despite the actions of some of her other family members. She's been a longtime, loyal employee of this bank, and not once has she given me any reason for concern."

"She's a McBride," Sam Jennings repeated, as if that fact was all he needed to support his opinion.

Wade studied the hostility in the balding, fifty-something dentist's eyes. "If the McBrides are so bad, why haven't I encountered any of them professionally during the time I've been here?"

"The McBrides aren't all bad," Hayes answered firmly. "Like all large families, they've had their share of problems...."

"The family includes a horse thief, more than a few drunks, a couple of sluts and a murderer," Jennings sneered. "An embezzler would fit right into that clan."

"Now that's just too much." Hayes looked as if moral outrage had finally overcome his financial discretion. "I find it almost impossible to believe that Emily is an embezzler. And there are some other fine, upstanding citizens among the McBride clan. Emily's uncle, Caleb McBride, and his wife, Bobbie, are pillars of their church and community. Their daughter went to Harvard Law School, one of their sons is a political bigwig in Washington and the other attends the Air Force Academy. You're basing your insinuations on a few totally unrelated incidents, Sam, and you'll be lucky if the whole McBride family doesn't sue you for slander."

"A horse thief?" Wade murmured, lifting an eyebrow at the irritated men.

The bank president snorted. "Three generations back, one of the McBrides was accused of being behind a horse-stealing ring. No one was ever able to prove it."

"Just like no one could prove Lucas McBride killed my nephew, Roger, fifteen years ago," Jennings snapped. "But everyone knows he did it."

Wade shook his head. "As interesting as all this family history is," he drawled, "it has little to do with the case at hand. What, specifically, are you claiming has happened, Dr. Jennings?"

Jennings sighed and rolled his eyes, then repeated his story slowly, as if he was speaking to a dim-witted child. "Three thousand dollars has disappeared from my business account. I've got records of it going in, but it wasn't on my statement."

"You made the deposits yourself?" Wade asked.

Jennings shook his head. "Of course not. My girl at the office handles deposits."

"And have you questioned her about the discrepancy?"

Jennings scowled. "The last one isn't with me anymore. I hired a new girl last week. She wouldn't know anything about it."

"What about the...er...girl who worked for you before? Have you talked to her?"

"She moved out of town. But if you're asking if I suspect her, you're off the mark. She worked for me for five years and never took a penny she didn't earn."

"Emily McBride has worked for *me* for almost seven years," Hayes retorted. "She's been responsible for a lot bigger accounts than yours, and there's never been a slip in her work."

"Not that you've caught, anyway," Jennings muttered.

Since the men seemed about ready to come to blows—verbal ones, at least—Wade decided it was time to intercede again.

"Suppose you call Ms. McBride in here and we'll talk with her a bit," he suggested to the bank president. He had met Emily McBride in the real-estate office yesterday afternoon—and if she was an embezzler, he'd eat his badge, he thought. His snap judgments were usually reliable.

Jennings looked startled by Wade's suggestion. "That's your idea of conducting a discreet investigation? You're just going to ask her if she's been stealing money from my account?"

Wade shrugged and reached into his pocket for a stick of gum. "I don't play a lot of cops-and-robbers games. Most times, the best way to come up with information is just to ask."

He didn't add that he'd seen more than a few amateur embezzlers break down and confess at the first accusation against them. Nor did he see any need to explain that he had a knack for sensing when someone was lying. And when he decided that they were, he had his own way of conducting investigations. Wade's methods of enforcing the law had never been strictly by the book, and that had gotten him into hot water on several occasions.

Hayes glared at both Jennings and Wade. "I won't have her browbeaten."

"Left my rubber hose back at the office," Wade assured him, unwrapping his gum.

Hayes didn't respond to the attempt at humor. He punched a button on the intercom sitting on his battered, antique-looking wooden desk and snapped, "Ann, ask Emily to come in here, please."

Wade folded the stick of gum in half and popped it into his mouth. There was an uneasy silence in the office for the three or four minutes that passed before someone tapped tentatively on the closed door.

Hayes walked around his desk and opened the door. "Come in, Emily."

Wade watched with interest as the woman Jennings had spoken of with such hostility—the woman Wade had met for the first time less than twenty-four hours ago—entered the room. She didn't look like an embezzler, he thought again. In fact, she looked like someone who should be selling complexion soap or toothpaste. Curly, golden-blond hair. Big blue eyes. Skin that was flawless except for a faint smattering of freckles that Wade found rather appealing. Girl-next-door smile. Average height. Better-than-average body, from what he could tell beneath her short-sleeve knit top and long, floral skirt.

Hayes began with a brusqueness that was probably intended to mask his discomfort with the situation. "Emily, you know Sam Jennings."

"Of course. How are you, Dr. Jennings?"

Wade noted that her smile was not reflected in her eyes as she greeted the man.

Jennings only grunted in response.

The animosity between them was obviously deep and long-standing.

Hayes motioned toward Wade, who was still leaning comfortably against the wall, his arms crossed over his uniformed chest. "Emily McBride, this is Chief of Police Wade Davenport."

Her big blue eyes turned inquiringly in Wade's direction. He found himself suddenly standing just a bit straighter.

"Yes, we've met. Good afternoon, Chief Davenport," she said, her tone only marginally warmer than it had been when she'd spoken to Jennings.

"The chief has some questions for you, Emily, if you don't mind," Hayes added.

"You have questions for *me*, Chief Davenport?"

"Actually, Dr. Jennings here has a few questions." Wade thought he might learn almost as much from Jenning's questions as from Emily McBride's answers.

Jennings huffed impatiently. "Now, you want *me* to do the questioning? Just what kind of police chief are you, anyway?"

"The only one you've got at the moment," Wade drawled, then motioned toward Emily McBride. "Go ahead, Jennings. Ask your questions."

EMILY WONDERED what in the world was going on. What could Sam Jennings possibly want to ask her that involved her boss? Suddenly she found herself getting nervous. What did they want from her, anyway? And why was the chief of police here?

She found it rather surprising that she reacted to the sight of him as intensely this time as she had the day before. She wasn't sure what it was about him that had immediately appealed to her, but she was definitely intrigued.

Jennings cleared his throat, drawing Emily's attention to his heavy, florid, scowling face. "I've got money missing out of my business account," he said without preface. "Three thousand dollars."

She waited for him to elaborate. When he didn't, she asked cautiously, "Are you saying that we've made an error in your account?"

He pointed to the computer monitor on Marshall Hayes's desk, and waved a stack of paper in his other hand. "According to your records, the amounts listed on these deposit slips were more than the amounts actually put into my account. It happened on several different deposits during eight weeks, so I find it hard to believe it was a simple error every time."

Emily frowned. Surely he wasn't suggesting...?

"Your initials are on all these deposit slips," he added aggressively.

She lifted her chin and narrowed her eyes. "Are you implying that I took money out of your deposits?"

He nodded. "Either that, or you are totally incompetent as a teller. Can't even write numbers down correctly."

Emily didn't get angry very often. In her family, it had been better just to quietly fade into the background when things got tense. Living in the shadow of her mother's sins and her brother's reputation, she had become an almost compulsive pleaser in order to be accepted in her town. And it had worked. People liked her. Maybe they used her a bit, but they treated her with courtesy, for the most part. They didn't humiliate her by making unjustified accusations against her, to her face and in front of witnesses.

At least, no one had before today.

Very aware that her employer and her town's chief of police were watching her, she tried to rein in her flare of temper and speak calmly and confidently. "Obviously, a mistake has been made somewhere, Dr. Jennings. But I can assure you, I have not deliberately taken any of your money, nor would I have made mistakes in your deposits on four separate occasions without catching and correcting them."

"I have deposit slips with your initials on them," he said again, fanning the air with the yellow paper rectangles. "And a statement that shows actual deposit amounts less than those written on the slips."

"May I see the slips?" Emily asked, still keeping her voice cool, though her anger was growing hotter. Why wasn't her boss defending her? Was the police chief waiting to arrest her? Why wasn't he saying anything?

She held out her hand. The heavy gold-link bracelet on her wrist clinked with the movement. Jennings looked at the bracelet and scowled, as if the frivolous sound made him even more annoyed than he already was.

Looking as though he expected her to destroy his "evidence" on the spot, he warily handed the four deposit slips and the bank statement to her. Emily glanced at them, then returned them to him. "Those deposit slips are fakes," she said without hesitation.

Jennings scowled. "I should have known you'd say something like that."

"Yes. You *should* have known I would tell the truth." She glanced at her boss. "I always stamp deposit slips with a date stamp. These slips aren't stamped, and I didn't write the initials on them. It isn't my handwriting."

Marshall Hayes smiled at her in a way that suggested he'd known all along that she was innocent of Jenning's charges. Or was she only seeing what she wanted to find in her employer's expression?

"Of course it's your handwriting. *E.McB.* That's the way you always initial your work. I checked," Jennings added a bit smugly.

"Then you should have noticed that I elevate the small *c* and put a dash beneath it," she retorted. "It's the way I've always signed my initials. The dash is missing on these. Why would I change my signature only on slips that I've supposedly falsified? That wouldn't make sense."

"I can bring in dozens of documents with her initials on them to verify her handwriting," Hayes offered.

The police chief cleared his throat. "Seems to me," he said, his voice a leisurely drawl, "we need to talk to your former employee, Dr. Jennings. It's entirely possible that she wrote out two deposit slips on these occasions. One with the correct amount on it for your records, another with the actual amount she deposited."

Jennings glared at him. "You're blaming my girl."

"I'm not blaming anyone—including Ms. McBride," the chief replied. "I'm simply saying we have to consider all the angles."

"I can produce paperwork proving I deposited the full amounts I was given," Emily volunteered, grateful that Davenport didn't seem to be in a hurry to haul her off to jail.

"It would be just as easy for you to fake paperwork as it would've been for Tammy," Jennings retorted.

Emily met his eyes without blinking. "But I didn't."

To her satisfaction, Jennings was the first to look

away. "You aren't going to do anything about this?" he demanded of Davenport.

The police chief nodded. "I'll look into it. I'll need the name and new address of your former employee, and of course I'll want to see all the paperwork."

"I—er—don't know where Tammy is now," Jennings muttered. "I've tried to contact her a couple of times, but I can't seem to locate her."

"Sounds to me like you've got a lot more reason to suspect Tammy than Emily," Marshall Hayes commented, giving her a reassuring nod.

Emily knew exactly why Sam Jennings would rather suspect her than his former employee. Emily was a McBride. Daughter of Nadine, sister of Lucas. That was reason enough for Sam Jennings to accuse her of all manner of sins.

She looked pointedly at her watch. "If there's nothing else I can do for you now, I need to get back to work. Friday afternoons are our busiest time."

"Go ahead, Emily," Hayes said promptly. "I think you've given us all the information we need for now, don't you agree, Chief?"

Davenport nodded, looking at Emily with thoughtful brown eyes. "Thank you for your cooperation, Ms. McBride. I'll be in touch if I need anything more."

"You're going to just let her go off and handle other people's money?" Jennings asked Hayes with a show of incredulity.

"Yes," the bank president answered. "I am. Chief?"

"I have no further reason to detain her," Davenport agreed, to Jennings's visible disgust. "I assume Dr. Jennings is aware that he shouldn't be publicly casting blame while the investigation is ongoing."

Jennings scowled.

Emily nodded, turned on one heel and left the office. She didn't speak to Sam Jennings on the way out. Nor did she look at the police chief again. But she was aware that both men watched her until she was out of their sight.

She could hardly take in the fact that she had just been accused of embezzlement. Surely no one who knew her could ever believe such a thing. And yet...she was a McBride. McBrides had been falsely accused before. Her brother Lucas. Her cousin Savannah. No one had believed claims of innocence from either of them.

Would anyone believe Emily if Sam Jennings persisted in his allegations? Or would they see her as just another McBride turned bad?

2

OLIVER WENT NUTS when Emily's doorbell rang Sunday afternoon, just before four o'clock. The little gray poodle yapped and bounced in front of the door, ferociously warning off potential invaders.

"As if you could do anything, anyway," Emily muttered, trying to step around the excited dog. "You don't even have any teeth, you silly old mutt."

She shifted the lace curtain over the triangular window in the old-fashioned front door so that she could look outside. Her eyes widened when she recognized the man on her doorstep. Her pulse fluttered, but she tried to write that off as uneasiness about his reasons for being there, rather than a reaction to his ruggedly attractive appearance.

"It's the cops, Oliver," she muttered with a grim attempt at humor. "Looks like we're busted."

She opened the door. "Are you here to arrest me, Chief Davenport?"

He gave her the lazy smile she remembered from their first meeting. "No, ma'am. I've just got a couple more questions for you, if you have the time."

Ignoring the poodle yipping frantically at her heels, Emily frowned. "Does this mean I'm still a suspect?"

Davenport shrugged one broad shoulder beneath the chambray shirt he wore with faded jeans—hardly standard police uniform. "I don't know that I would go that far," he replied. "But you are an integral part of an ongoing investigation."

She frowned. "That sounds to me like a fancy way of saying I'm a suspect."

His sudden smile took her breath away. The man was entirely too attractive for her peace of mind, especially considering his reason for being on her doorstep.

"Is this a good time to ask a few questions?" he asked, nodding toward the door in an obvious hint.

Somewhat suspiciously, Emily studied Wade's pleasant, friendly-looking expression. Finding nothing there to alarm her, she sighed faintly and reacted the way she always did when townspeople showed up on her doorstep. She held the door open.

"I suppose this is as good a time as any. Won't you come in, Chief Davenport?"

Wade promptly took her up on the invitation.

WADE COULDN'T HELP noticing that Emily McBride's living room looked as though it belonged to a little old lady, not the attractive young woman she was. He doubted that the decor had been changed in the past twenty years, if not more.

He'd done his research since meeting her. He knew Emily had grown up in this house. That her father had left his entire estate—little as it was reported to be—to Emily when he'd died less than six months ago. He was also aware that it was not yet common knowledge in Honoria that Emily had listed the house for sale.

Wade glanced around the room with the eyes of a potential buyer. He'd been renting a little bungalow since moving to Honoria four months ago, hoping to find a house to buy, but nothing had appealed to him yet. Emily McBride's place interested him—almost as much as she did.

The house sat on twenty acres of mostly wooded property, seven miles out of town. The yard surrounding the frame structure was a good size. Needed some landscaping work done, but very nice, on the whole. The house itself was white, wood-sided, with big, black-shuttered windows and a wide, wraparound porch. Four bedrooms and two baths, according to the Realtor. A large, open living area with a fireplace. Probably a big kitchen. The house, too, could use some work—just general maintenance things Wade could do himself, for the most part—but it looked to be in pretty good shape. It was a house meant for a family.

Wade could picture himself living here with his son.

A wheezy, overweight gray poodle that had to be fifteen years old, at least, danced noisily around Wade.

"Be quiet, Oliver," Emily ordered sharply.

The dog subsided into disgruntled rumbles. Wade had always thought poodles were pleasant, good-natured dogs, but this one had him revising his opinion.

Emily motioned toward a comfortable-looking sofa. "Please have a seat, Chief Davenport. I have iced tea, or I can make a pot of coffee, if you'd like some."

"Iced tea sounds good." Feeling a bit like a bull in a china shop, he made his way around a table loaded with fragile bric-a-brac.

"I'll be right back." She turned and hurried out of the room.

Wade watched her until she was out of sight—she looked darned good in her jeans, he couldn't help noticing—and then turned his attention back to her living space, ignoring the dog who stood guard at the doorway.

An antique cherry sideboard against the wall nearest the sofa was particularly interesting. It was covered with photographs. Dozens of them. Old sepia-toned portraits. Newer, color studio poses. Framed snapshots—black-and-white from decades past, color shots that looked much more recent. There were pictures of children, teenagers, adults, family groups, even a portrait of a beautiful Irish setter. There were no photos of the irritable poodle.

The collection had obviously been arranged by someone to whom family was very important. Was Emily the one who'd assembled all these photos, or had it been started by her parents? And if she was the one who so carefully maintained the collection, why was she selling her family home?

Wade was finding Emily McBride more interesting with every observation he made of her, and with every snippet of information anyone had told him about her.

Emily returned carrying a tray that held two glasses of iced tea and a plate of assorted cookies. She set it carefully on the low table in front of Wade, then took a seat on a small chair facing him. "Now," she said, "what can I do for you, Chief Davenport?"

The totally inappropriate replies that popped immediately into Wade's mind startled him.

Stick to the job, Davenport, he reminded himself irritably.

"First," he said, "I want to apologize for that awkward scene in your employer's office. I'm not sure I handled that very well."

She frowned, but lifted one shoulder in a slight shrug. "You probably had little choice. I know what Sam Jennings can be like."

"Yeah, well, I'm just learning. Coming into a new town, there's a lot to understand about the people here. Like the interpersonal relationships, for example."

"Is that a fancy way of saying 'family feuds'?" she asked wryly. "I'm surprised you didn't learn about the bad blood between the McBrides and the Jennings as soon as you walked into your office the first day."

Wade hadn't heard about it quite that early, but he'd been told a fair bit since Jennings had made his accusations on Friday. Now he wanted to hear about it from Emily. "Just how long has this 'feud' been going on?"

"Since long before I was born. I think it started with my great-grandfather and Sam Jennings's grandfather. It's been going on in one way or another ever since. It's, um, particularly ugly when it comes to my branch of the family."

"Sam Jennings has a reason to want to hurt you, personally?" Wade had already wondered if Jennings disliked Emily enough to plant evidence of a crime against her. The animosity that Sam had shown toward Emily in the bank president's office had seemed totally out of proportion to the unsubstantiated accusations he'd made against her.

"Sam hated my father. I think Sam may have dated my mother when they were in high school, but I don't know if that was the entire problem. My father wouldn't talk about the Jennings family." She drew a deep breath, then added, "My mother ran off with Sam's older brother when I was little more than a baby.

Al Jennings was also married, and the father of two children at the time. No one has heard from him or my mother in the past twenty-four years. I don't even know if they're still alive."

Emily presented those unpleasant facts with a firmly lifted chin, but her eyes spoke of the heartache of an abandoned little girl. Wade doubted that she realized quite how much those big, blue eyes of hers revealed— or how deeply he reacted to the echoes of her pain.

"I'm sorry," he said, knowing the words were inadequate.

She shrugged and glanced away. "I figured you would hear about it, if you haven't already. It was quite a scandal. My mother was the town hussy—apparently she dated most of the single men and a few of the married ones before she married my father, and then she abandoned my father, my brother and me to run off with yet another married man. Ten years later, my brother was accused of murdering that man's son."

Her flat, unemotional tone didn't match the starkly appalling words.

Wade had heard the whispers that Emily McBride's older brother had gotten away with murder fifteen years ago. After meeting Emily in the bank, he'd gone back to his office and looked up the old files. There hadn't been much in them. The chief of police at that time had investigated the death of twenty-one-year-old Roger Jennings, who'd fallen—either accidentally or through foul play—from a thirty-foot bluff on McBride land, in the woods behind this house.

There'd been testimony of years of active animosity between Lucas McBride and Roger Jennings, even a witness who'd heard McBride threaten Jennings's life.

There'd been notes about twenty-year-old McBride's notorious temper, and his two previous arrests for fighting. But there'd been no solid evidence to charge him with Roger Jennings's death. McBride had had an alibi—a nineteen-year-old girl who claimed he'd spent the entire night with her. But many had suggested that girl would have said anything Lucas McBride asked her to. There had apparently been a few inconsistencies in the girl's testimony, but not enough to form a basis for an arrest.

Chief Packer had written "Unsolved" on the case file. And two months after Roger Jennings died in that mysterious fall, Lucas left town in the middle of the night. He was the second member of Emily's family to do so, it seemed. Wade couldn't help wondering what those desertions must have done to a vulnerable little girl.

Emily McBride wasn't a little girl now. A woman faced him with shadows in her eyes, hard-won pride in her posture, anxiety and defiance warring in her expression.

She fascinated him. Which wasn't a good thing, considering that he had a job to do and she was a suspect—no matter that Wade considered her an unlikely one.

"Have you personally had any conflicts with Sam Jennings?" he asked.

"No. He glares at me whenever our paths cross, but he glares at all of us, including my Uncle Caleb and Aunt Bobbie, the only other McBrides still living in Honoria. He just can't stand our family."

"And what about the other members of the Jennings family? Do they glare at the McBrides, as well?"

"There aren't that many of them left around here, either," Emily admitted. "Sam's been divorced a couple of times. No kids. His brother, of course, ran off with my mother. The wife Al Jennings deserted moved away with her daughter about a year after her son, Roger, died in an accident that some people tried to blame on my brother. There may be a couple of distant cousins still around, but no one who was as personally involved in all the tragedies as Sam."

"What about Sam Jennings's former office assistant? Did she have any reason to dislike you?"

"Tammy Powell?" Emily frowned as she said the name, then shook her head, her blond curls swaying around her face with the motion. "No, not that I'm aware of. I didn't really know her very well. She was in the bank often, of course, but we usually only exchanged pleasantries, nothing more. We weren't friends, but we weren't enemies, either. Just acquaintances."

"I've sent out some inquiries about her. She left no forwarding address when she left town."

"That's strange," Emily mused with a frown. "She lived here for quite a while. Her grandparents still live in the country about fifteen miles out of Honoria."

"They claim they don't know where she is, but that she promised to let them know as soon as she settled somewhere."

"Unlike Sam Jennings, I don't like blaming someone without evidence, but I did not initial the deposit slips he showed me in Mr. Hayes's office. If Tammy is the one who signed those slips with my initials, then she obviously took some of her employer's money with her when she left town."

Wade privately believed that was exactly what had happened. But he wasn't prepared just yet to announce that conclusion aloud.

He tried to convince himself that he was *not* using this investigation as an excuse to spend more time getting to know Emily McBride. That would be unprofessional, and despite his sometimes unorthodox methods, he had always been a professional. But the investigation was ongoing, so he would certainly be seeing Emily again—which, he had to admit, would be a pleasure, as far as he was concerned.

"Maybe you should just put this out of your mind for a few days while I try to locate Tammy Powell," he advised her.

"Put it out of my mind?" Emily stared at him in disbelief. "I've been publicly accused of embezzlement, and you think I should just put it out of my mind?"

He lifted a hand in a conciliatory gesture. "I'm sorry. I know this is upsetting for you...."

"Slightly," she muttered.

"But," he continued with a chiding look at her, "I had a long talk with Dr. Jennings and asked him not to repeat his accusations to anyone else without further proof. I reminded him that you could always sue him for defamation of character if he continues to slander you without evidence...and especially if it turns out that his former employee was the embezzler, after all. I think he paid attention to my warning."

Emily studied Wade's face for so long that he had to resist the impulse to squirm self-consciously on her sofa. "You really don't think I had anything to do with this, do you?"

He couched his answer carefully. "Obviously, I have

to look at all the facts before I draw any conclusions. But if it makes you feel any better, I consider you an unlikely suspect at this point."

"So why did you come here today?"

Because I wanted to see you again. The truth flashed through Wade's thoughts so clearly that he wondered for a moment if he'd spoken aloud.

He cleared his throat. "I guess I just wanted to confirm some hunches."

Her blue eyes didn't waver, making him even more conscious of being pinned in her perceptive gaze. "Do you always operate on hunches, Chief Davenport?"

"It's only one of my methods," he said, giving her a slight smile.

After a moment, Emily looked away. "Well, I'm glad your hunch leans in my favor this time."

Lady, you have no idea.

EMILY COULDN'T HELP noticing that the police chief seemed to be in no hurry to leave her living room. He took his time sipping his tea and eating cookies, looking as though there was nowhere else he needed to be anytime soon.

"Good cookie," he said, nodding in approval.

Watching Wade with greedy eyes, the overweight poodle made a sound that closely resembled a belch, then looked at the plate of cookies and whined.

"You aren't getting cookies, Oliver," Emily said sternly. "You're too fat already."

"Have you had the dog long?" Wade asked, looking curiously from Emily to Oliver.

"About three hours," Emily answered wryly. "I'm dog-sitting."

Wade chuckled. "That explains it, then."

"Explains what?"

He nodded toward the bad-tempered poodle. "I was having a little trouble imagining you with this dog. It just didn't seem to fit."

"I'm afraid Oliver has been overly indulged," Emily agreed wryly. "I'm fond of dogs, in general, but like children, they can be terribly spoiled if they aren't given boundaries."

Wade swallowed the last bite of his cookie, then asked, "Do you like children?"

"When they're housebroken," she replied. And then she laughed softly and admitted, "Actually, I love children. My cousin Savannah has thirteen-year-old twins. And my cousin Trevor has an adorable two-year-old son. They all live out of town, but I see them as often as I get the chance."

Wade looked around the spacious living room again, and she saw him take note of the old-fashioned high ceilings and wood-sashed windows. Again, that funny, hollow feeling came over her when she thought of him living in her house.

"This looks like a great place to raise kids," he murmured.

She nodded. "My cousins and I loved playing in our woods when we were young."

Memories flashed in swift succession through her mind. Burying the time capsule with Savannah and Tara. Climbing trees with Tara's brothers, Trevor and Trent, who'd been only a couple of years younger than Emily. Fishing in the shallow creek with Lucas.

The unbidden thought of her half brother made her wince. She had unabashedly idolized him. She had treasured those afternoons when he'd indulged her by taking her fishing or to afternoon movies.

"How old is the house?" Wade asked, breaking into the bittersweet memories.

"Almost forty years. My father built it when he married his first wife."

Wade's expression was somber. "You said your father died recently?"

Emily saw the warm sympathy in his eyes, and felt an urge to be honest with him. "Dad died in May. He was ill for a very long time, and he didn't speak or recognize anyone for the last few years of his life. His death finally put him at peace."

And then she decided that she'd talked more than enough about her family to this man. She wouldn't mind turning the tables a bit.

"So you want to buy a house," she said. "Does that mean you like living in Honoria?"

"Very much," he answered with a smile. "I've been pretty busy, settling into the new job and all, but everyone's been real nice and neighborly, for the most part."

"Where did you live before you moved here?"

"I've been with Atlanta CID—Criminal Investigations Division—for the past few years."

Atlanta. Big. Fast-paced. Busy. A far cry from sleepy little Honoria. "This town must seem awfully dull, compared to Atlanta. You probably won't see as many crimes in a year here as you did in a few weeks there."

"I hope not," he said fervently. "I grew up in a little town in Alabama that was a lot like this one. When I started looking for a new position last year, this is exactly what I was hoping to find. I can do the job I was trained for here, but still have time to relax and spend time with my son."

"How old is he?"

"Eight. And a half, as he always points out."

Emily ran a fingertip around the rim of her glass. "He's your only child?"

"Yes. But he's a fine one," he added with a proud-papa grin.

She smiled. "I'm sure he is."

Oliver coughed wheezily and rubbed his nose against one paw.

"Sounds like he's got a cold coming on," Wade commented.

Emily had a sudden clutch of panic. "If he gets sick...or worse...while Martha and Arthur Godwin are on their cruise..." She shuddered, not even wanting to think about that possibility.

Wade whipped his head around to stare at her. "This dog belongs to the Godwins?"

She nodded.

Wade seemed to struggle against a grin. And then he burst into a full-bodied laugh that made Emily smile in response. "Now *that* fits," he said. "No wonder you've found yourself with this mutt on your hands. Who could say no to Martha Godwin?"

"I guess that's one local citizen you're getting to know quite well."

"You could say so. She seems to be in my office every other day. I understand she's usually in the mayor's office on alternate days."

"Martha likes to stay involved in the community," Emily said, stifling a smile.

"She's an...interesting woman."

Emily glanced at Oliver. "Yes. She is."

Wade glanced at his watch. Emily thought there was just a hint of reluctance in his voice when he said, "I suppose I'd better be going. I'm sure you have things to do."

She didn't, but she saw no need to tell him that. She set her tea glass on a coaster and rose. "You'll let me know the status of your investigation, Chief Davenport?"

He nodded as he stood. "Of course. Try not to worry about it. But...er...you should probably stay in town until everything is settled."

The words hit her like a slap in the face, though he'd obviously tried to phrase the instructions carefully. She'd been lulled into thinking of him as a friendly visitor. She'd forgotten that he still considered her a suspect in an embezzlement case. And his order for her not to go anywhere brought back that suffocating feeling of being trapped in this house, in this town.

She saw him to the door. He stood on the porch a moment, and she could tell that he was still assessing the place. She didn't quite know how to feel about that, since she hadn't yet actually shown the house to prospective buyers.

But this was what she wanted to do, she reminded herself. What she'd been wanting to do for years. It was only deep-seated nostalgia—and general annoyance with him—that was making her suddenly have to fight the urge to tell Wade Davenport that he could stop eyeing *her* house.

"Would you mind very much if I make an appointment to come back soon with the Realtor?" he asked, turning to her with that lazy smile that made her insides quiver in an oddly disturbing manner.

"No, of course not." She hoped he wasn't perceptive enough to notice that her own smile was patently false. "I would show you around now, but—"

He held up a hand, obviously a characteristic gesture for him. "No, I won't put you to that trouble without notice this way. I'll go through the regular channels. Thank you for taking the time to talk to me...Ms. Mc-Bride."

Something in his deep drawl made the formal address seem more intimate than it should have. Or was her imagination getting away from her?

She wasn't sure what to do or say. Falling back on deeply ingrained manners, she stuck out her right hand. "Good afternoon, Chief Davenport."

His hand swallowed hers. His palm was roughened by hard work, and very warm against her chilled skin. And she felt her knees go shaky in reaction.

She'd never responded like this to a simple handshake. She couldn't imagine what would happen if this man should ever kiss her....

What was she thinking? A kiss between her and the chief of police—a family man, she reminded herself—was never going to happen.

She removed her hand hastily from his. "Goodbye," she said, and closed the door between them with somewhat more haste than courtesy.

WADE LOOKED at that closed door for a moment with a lifted eyebrow. And then he glanced down at his right hand, which still seemed to be tingling from contact with hers.

He was whistling between his teeth when he climbed into his Jeep and started the engine.

He would definitely be seeing Emily McBride again.

3

ALWAYS ON THE FIRST Saturday in October, the towns-people of Honoria gathered at Sidney Applegate Park for a festival to mark the symbolic end of summer. Hot dogs and hamburgers sizzled fragrantly on grills manned by city dignitaries. Vendors sold ice cream and sodas and snow cones. There was an antique-car show, and a cutest-pet show. Local merchants sponsored booths advertising their services with giveaway items. Amusement-park rides, games of chance, pony rides, a storytelling circle, and other attractions were set up for the children.

Emily had been "volunteered" to work the face-painting booth for a local civic club.

Several squirming children stood at her elbow as she put the finishing touches to a cluster of colorful balloons on a little girl's chubby cheek. Emily had promised to work another half hour at this booth, and then she was taking a break—whether anyone replaced her or not, she thought firmly. She'd already supervised the beanbag-tossing game and she'd promised to help judge the baking contest later.

Just ask Emily, she thought wryly. The unofficial town motto. It should be emblazoned on the sign that marked the city limits of Honoria.

Five minutes before Emily's shift ended, a little boy

with blazing red hair and an adorably snub nose slipped into the metal chair in front of her. And then he just sat there, studying her solemnly.

"Would you like your face painted?" she asked him with a smile, struck by the gravity of his round blue eyes.

The boy nodded.

She showed him the chart that held the available designs. Balloons, hearts, rainbows, flowers, a few popular cartoon figures, smiley faces, Superman's *S* and Batman's bat symbol were among the choices. "Which one do you want?"

The little boy studied the chart closely, biting his lip, as if the decision was terribly important. Emily waited patiently.

Finally, the boy pointed to a picture. "That one," he said in little more than a whisper.

The drawing he'd selected was a fat goldfish with blue bubbles rising from its smiling mouth. It would be the first of its kind that Emily had done, but the sketch looked simple enough. "All right. What's your name?"

"Clay."

"Do you like fish, Clay?" she asked, reaching for the paint pens.

He nodded.

"Do you have a goldfish?"

Another nod.

"What's your fish's name?"

"Moby."

Emily smiled. "That's very cute."

"He's named after a whale in a book," the child volunteered. "My daddy told me about him."

Emily traced the outline of the cartoon fish on the

boy's impossibly soft cheek. "Yes, I've heard of Moby Dick, the white whale in the story."

"My daddy said the whale was ferocious. But my Moby's a nice fish."

Emily was amused at the child's mature manner. *What a sweetheart.* "Is your Moby all gold or does he have spots?" she asked, thinking she'd make the cartoon fish as close to his pet as possible without seeing it.

"He's orange. All orange."

"I see." Emily reached for the orange paint pen.

"I'm here to relieve you, Emily," a young woman said, setting her purse on the table at Emily's elbow.

"Thanks, Grace. Let me finish this one, and then I'll get out of your way."

"You're lookin' good, Sparky," Grace said, studying the little boy's partially painted cheek.

He blinked. "My name's not Sparky. It's Clay."

Emily laughed. "That's okay, Clay. She calls all the guys 'Sparky.'"

"Only the cute ones," Grace said flippantly.

Emily drew a trail of tiny blue bubbles around the happy-looking fish, then leaned back to admire her work. "It does look good, if I do say so myself. Want to see it, Clay?"

He nodded eagerly. She gave him a hand mirror.

Clay peered into the glass, then broke into a broad grin that warmed Emily's heart. "It looks just like Moby!"

Emily loved children. All children. She had actually enjoyed her stint at the face-painting booth, and had been amused by all the little ones she'd chatted with that afternoon. But this child touched her in a special way. There was something about that grave little face of his...or maybe that heartbreaker smile.

"Hey, pal. Looks like you're all decorated."

Emily looked quickly over her shoulder in response to the familiar male voice coming from behind her. Chief of Police Wade Davenport stood close by, thumbs hooked in the belt loops of the faded jeans he wore with a khaki police-uniform shirt. It was the first time she'd seen him since he'd stopped by her house last Sunday.

The bright sun reflected from the badge he wore on his chest. He wasn't wearing a weapon, only a walkie-talkie clipped to his belt, but he looked tough and official, nevertheless—except for the softness in his eyes when he smiled at young Clay.

This adorable little boy was the police chief's son?

Confirming her startled realization, the child said, "Daddy, look what this lady painted on my face. It's Moby!"

"Well, it sure is. Looks just like him."

Clay beamed.

Suddenly self-conscious, Emily stood to allow Grace to take over her spot, and the line of increasingly restless children waiting to be painted. Her movement drew Wade's attention.

He smiled at her. "Afternoon, Ms. McBride," he drawled.

"Chief Davenport," she responded with a slight nod of her head.

Grace grinned irreverently as she slid into the seat Emily had vacated. "Want *your* face painted, Sparky?" she asked the police chief. "I'd be happy to oblige."

"I think I'll pass," he answered good-naturedly. "But thanks for the offer."

Emily thought that Grace's expression offered a lot more than a cheek painting, but Wade seemed oblivious to the implications.

"Is your shift over?" he asked Emily, falling into step beside her as she walked away from the booth.

She nodded. "I've been sitting there so long that I need to walk around a bit."

His little hand swallowed in his father's much bigger one, Clay peered up at Emily through his long, curling lashes. "You could walk with us," he suggested, his expression shy.

"Well, I—"

"Actually," Wade said, breaking into Emily's intended polite refusal, "you could do us a favor, Ms. McBride. If you don't mind Ferris wheels, that is."

She lifted an eyebrow. Had the police chief already figured out the unwritten town motto? "What do you mean?"

Wade's expression turned sheepish. "Clay, here, has been begging me to take him on the Ferris wheel. I—er—wondered if you'd mind riding it with him. Unless heights bother you, of course," he added hastily.

"I love the Ferris wheel," Emily replied with a quick smile at the boy, who gazed up at her hopefully. "I'd be happy to ride with you, Clay."

"Really?" He looked delighted. "I've been wishing and wishing to ride it, but Daddy's scared."

Wade's cheeks were a shade darker when Emily shot him a surprised look. "I—er—sorta have this thing about heights," he admitted. "I can deal with it if I have to, but it's not something I choose to do for fun."

Emily might have teased him about it had Clay not been there. But she wouldn't say anything to embarrass him in front of his obviously adoring son.

She was rather startled when Clay slid his free hand into hers, linking the three of them as they strolled along the crowded sidewalk. Emily was uncomfortably aware that she'd immediately become the object of speculation by the townspeople who noticed them, but she had no intention of rejecting the child's friendly gesture. Putting potential gossip out of her head as best as she could, she smiled down at the boy and lightly squeezed his fingers.

It was unseasonably warm in the park, with the afternoon sun blazing overhead and the crowds bumping elbows on the sidewalk. Emily was glad she'd dressed coolly in a loose-fitting denim scoop-neck dress and leather sandals. Though schools had been open for a month and Halloween was only weeks away, summer heat still had a strong hold on Honoria.

The pet show had apparently just ended. Several dogs on leashes, from pedigreed champions to lovably homely mutts, were led past them. Emily couldn't help smiling at a slightly overweight boxer that seemed to wear a permanent grin on his ugly face. She didn't know if he'd won any awards for being cute, but he was certainly appealing in his own way.

And then a woman walked past with a glossy red chicken in her arms. The chicken wore a blue mesh collar with an attached leash, and was looking around as if it thoroughly enjoyed the surrounding festivities. Emily blinked, then looked automatically at Wade, who was grinning broadly as he unwrapped a stick of gum.

"Was that a chicken on a leash?" he asked.

"Yes, I believe it was," she replied just as gravely.

"So just where would one buy a collar and leash for a chicken?"

"At a chicken-and-dressing store," Clay said with a giggle.

"Now that's just sick," Wade said, his smile deepening.

Emily laughed, thinking that it was a very clever joke from such a little boy.

"There's the Ferris wheel!" Bouncing in excitement, Clay pointed upward.

Wade looked up, and Emily would have sworn he paled. "You're—uh—sure you want to do this, Clay?"

Clay nodded emphatically. "I want to see the park from up there."

"He'll be fine," Emily said reassuringly. "We'll be strapped in, and I'll hold on to him."

Wade looked at Emily, his expression suddenly speculative. "Maybe I should reconsider riding it. Would you hold on to me, too?"

She gulped as she realized that the chief of police had just made a not-so-subtle verbal pass at her. "I—uh—"

And then he laughed. She told herself he must have been teasing. The chief apparently had an odd sense of humor.

She was relieved when he turned away from her to step up to the window of the ticket booth. "Two tickets for the Ferris wheel, please," he requested.

Tickets in hand, Emily and Clay moved to the back of the line waiting to ride. A man with a graying braid and a beer belly under his T-shirt stood in line in front of them. Emily was startled to realize that the man was carrying a live green parrot on his shoulder.

"Clay, look," she said.

At the sound of her voice, the man turned and grinned down at Clay. "How ya' doin'?"

"You have a parrot on your shoulder!" Clay said, his blue eyes very round.

Looking comically startled, the man turned his head. "Well, danged if I don't."

Emily laughed. She had just read the wording on the guy's T-shirt. "Happiness is biting my parrot back." Wade, she suspected, would call it sick. But funny.

"Is your parrot going to ride the Ferris wheel?" Clay asked curiously.

"Oh, yeah. He loves the rides. 'Specially the merry-go-round."

"What's his name?"

"Vincent. And I'm Gus. What's *your* handle?"

Clay looked confused.

"He means your name," Emily prompted.

"Oh. My name's Clay."

Gus eyed the boy's face. "Hey, Clay. Did you know you've got a fish on your cheek?"

"Well, danged if I don't," Clay said, and then giggled.

This, Emily thought, was a seriously cute little boy.

Gus was still laughing when he turned to get onto the Ferris wheel with his parrot. Emily and Clay were ushered to the next available seat.

Minutes later they were climbing high in the air. With the safety belt fastened snugly around his waist and Emily's hand clamped just as tightly on his shoulder, Clay looked down in delight as his father got smaller and smaller below them.

"Daddy looks so little from up here. And look at the cars in the parking lot. They look like my Hot Wheels toys."

Pleased with the child's enthusiasm, Emily tried to respond to his excited comments whenever he gave her a chance to speak. To the boy's further delight, they stopped at the very top of the ride, where the car rocked gently while riders at the bottom were unloaded.

"Look at Daddy," Clay said, leaning as far over the safety rail as his seat belt and Emily's hand would let him.

Emily had been watching Wade Davenport since the ride had begun. And she was all too aware that he'd been watching her, too.

Or rather, he'd been watching his son, she corrected herself carefully. Wade certainly had no particular interest in her, other than as a suspect in an embezzlement case. Even if he had—jokingly, she was sure—made a pass at her.

Clay's painted face was radiant when the ride came to an end. "That was so cool. Thank you, Ms. McBride."

"You're very welcome. I enjoyed it, too. And why don't you call me Emily?" she suggested, feeling as if she'd made a new friend.

"Okay, Miss Emily," Clay said contentedly, proving that her new friend was most definitely a child of the Old South.

They held hands as they wound their way through the crowds and back to where Wade waited for them.

Clay released Emily and dashed to his father's side, telling him all about how his stomach had fluttered when the ride revolved and how tiny everything had looked from so high in the air.

Wade glanced at Emily with a wry smile. "The boy's easily entertained."

"The boy is delightful," she assured him. "We had a great time."

"Did you thank Ms. McBride for taking you on the ride?" Wade prompted his son.

"He thanked me very nicely," Emily answered for the child, who nodded in agreement.

Clay tugged at his father's hand. "I'm hungry, Daddy."

"Of course you are. You're awake, aren't you?"

Clay rolled his eyes as if he'd heard that response many times before. "Can we get something to eat?"

"Sure. Let's go check out the food stands. There are some pretty good smells coming from that direction."

Clay agreed, then gave Emily another of his endearingly shy smiles. "Will you come with us, Miss Emily?"

"Yes, please do, Miss Emily," Wade seconded, a teasing glint in his brown eyes.

"Thank you, but I'd better not. I'm judging a baking contest in a few minutes and I don't want to be too full to enjoy it."

Clay looked disappointed, but Wade only nodded. "Then we'll be seeing you around."

He and his son both thanked her again, which was becoming rather embarrassing since she'd enjoyed the ride almost as much as Clay had. And then Wade and

Clay headed toward the food stands. Clay looked over his shoulder to wave at Emily. Wade didn't look back.

With a somewhat wistful sigh, Emily turned away, only to be immediately hailed by someone she knew. And she braced herself for the inevitable questions about why she had looked so cozy with the police chief and his son.

A FIGHT BEGAN when April Penny's chewy-chocolate-cherry brownies lost out to Earlene Smithee's peaches-and-cream trifle in the baking contest.

Emily wasn't certain exactly what happened. One moment she was announcing the winner, and holding up the blue ribbon to be awarded to Mrs. Smithee. The next, she was standing beside the table of baked goods with peaches-and-cream trifle spattered on the front of her dress while April Penny and Earlene Smithee tried to claw each other's eyes out.

Emily hadn't realized that Wade Davenport was nearby until he came forward to break up the fracas.

"Okay, ladies, let's cool down a bit," he said, trying to step between the brawling matrons.

He got hit in the cheek with a handful of chewy-chocolate-and-cherry brownies.

"She rigged the contest!" April Penny shouted, pointing at her opponent with a chocolate-stained hand. "She always makes sure she wins."

"You just can't admit you lost—*again!*" Earlene retorted, her flushed face dotted with peaches.

April launched herself at her rival. Wade caught her neatly in one arm, preventing her from reaching her intended target.

"April, the contest was not rigged," Emily said, trying to be heard over the scandalized chattering around them. "It couldn't be. We had no idea who'd baked what until we opened the envelopes after the judging was finished."

The two other judges, a tiny, gray-haired school-teacher and a nervous-looking town councilman who'd been standing well back from the flying food and fists, both nodded fervently.

April sniffed, giving Emily a cold look. "I wouldn't be surprised if you had something to do with this. A McBride would do just about anything to keep me from winning."

Swiping ineffectively at the mess on the front of her dress, Emily shook her head, trying very hard to hold on to her temper. She reminded herself that she was in a public place. That she detested ugly scenes. And that she had no intention of sinking to April's usual level. "You're wrong, April," she said evenly. "Earlene won fairly."

April had always had a reputation for losing all discretion when in a temper, but her eyes were wilder than Emily had ever seen them when she snarled, "I suppose you expect me to take the word of a McBride. Cheating is just another talent of your whoring, murdering clan. And, according to Sam Jennings, you fit right in with the rest of them. Found any extra thousands lying around lately, Emily?"

A gasp came from the crowd of scandalized onlookers. Emily didn't have enough breath even to gasp. April's vicious verbal attack had knocked it right out of her. No one had *ever* spoken to her that way in public before! Or in private, for that matter. A red haze of anger clouded her vision and she moved instinctively forward. She didn't have to take this, she thought, her entire body quivering with rage.

Someone caught her arm. "Emily," her Aunt Bobbie murmured warningly. "Take a deep breath, dear."

It took several deep breaths, and a few more soothing words from her sympathetic aunt before Emily could regain control of herself. With one last, scathing look at April, she deliberately turned her back on the other woman. "Thank you, Aunt Bobbie. I'm fine now."

Muttering beneath her breath, April shook off Wade's restraining hand. "I'm getting out of here."

"That sounds like a good idea," Wade agreed, his voice cooler than Emily had heard it before.

April turned on one too-high sandal heel and stalked away, her rounded hips swaying markedly in her too-tight denim shorts.

"That woman," Earlene sniffed, tossing her bleached-blond head. "She's hated me ever since I beat her in the Miss Honoria pageant twenty years ago. You'd think she'd get over it, but no. She's still trying to outdo me."

She walked away, surrounded by friends and sympathizers.

"Well, our ungracious loser didn't sound overly fond of *you*, either," Wade murmured to Emily, moving to where she stood with her aunt.

"April's maiden name was Hankins," Emily explained, her voice still a bit higher pitched than usual. "There's a rather unpleasant history between the Hankins and the McBrides."

Wade chuckled wryly. "Are the McBrides involved in any other feuds I should know about?"

"Probably," Emily replied, unable to find any humor in the situation. "But I can't think of them at the moment."

Bobbie McBride shook her head as she took in the mess around them. "I can't believe the way April acted. She should be ashamed of herself."

"It's not the first time April has shown her butt in public," an older woman muttered, overhearing. "Remember that New Year's Eve she thought her husband was flirting with Melba Sands? Fur was sure flying that night."

Several other townspeople gathered around Bobbie to exchange avid gossip about April's shenanigans. Wrinkling her nose in distaste, Emily moved away from the group. Wade followed.

"Where's Clay?" she asked, relieved that the child hadn't been exposed to the ugly scene.

"He found one of his buddies from school. The other boy's mother took them to watch the magic show at the pavilion. I thought I'd wander around and soak up some of the local atmosphere. I guess I got a little more than I'd bargained for," he added, wiping chocolate-brownie crumbs off his face.

Emily finally managed a smile. "You look like you've been to the face-painting booth," she remarked, pulling a clean tissue out of her purse and dabbing at the smear of chocolate still decorating Wade's cheek. "I'm not sure what this is supposed to represent, though. It's definitely not a goldfish."

Wade stood very still beneath her ministrations. Emily suddenly became aware of her actions.

What was she doing? Without even stopping to think, she'd started wiping Wade's face as if he were no older than his son. She was standing only inches away from him, and it probably looked as if she was all but throwing herself in his arms.

Hastily, she stepped back. "That's—um, that's better."

"Thank you." Something in his eyes, and in the husky edge to his voice, made her face warm.

"I'd better be going," she said, stuffing the chocolate-stained tissue back into her purse and avoiding Wade's eyes. She glanced nervously at her food-stained dress. "I want to get out of these clothes."

And then she almost groaned as she realized what she'd said. She had a lamentable tendency to babble idiotically when she was nervous—as she'd just proven.

Wade's grin had a hint of devilry beneath it, though his voice was exaggeratedly innocent when he said, "Sounds like a good idea to me."

She told herself the double entendre was only in her own mind. But she couldn't really convince herself this time. She wasn't too naive to know when she was being flirted with—and Chief Wade Davenport had been subtly flirting with her all day.

Muttering something that was probably incomprehensible, she turned and headed rapidly toward the parking lot. Several acquaintances tried to delay her along the way, many wanting juicy details about the baking-contest squabble, but she evaded them skillfully, claiming weariness and her mussed dress as excuses.

"But, Emily, I wanted you to help me with the..."

Emily didn't slow down long enough to find out what one of her neighbors wanted her to do now. Whatever it was, this time she wouldn't do it.

Starting today, the citizens of Honoria were going to have to ask someone else to do their favors.

TUESDAY MORNING'S newspaper contained some disturbing information for the residents of crime-free Honoria. Three homes had been broken into the day before, while the owners were attending the annual fall festival at the park. The burglars had been swift and efficient, taking TVs, VCRs, jewelry, cash and other valuables and leaving no clues.

Police Chief Davenport, when contacted late Monday evening, just before the paper went to press, had informed the reporter that the break-ins would be thoroughly investigated and home-security patrols would be increased. "We will not tolerate this criminal behavior in our jurisdiction," he assured the residents of his new hometown.

Emily sighed and clucked her tongue. "What is this world coming to?" she asked Oliver, who sat at her feet begging for a piece of toast. "A law-abiding citizen can't feel safe in his own home these days."

And then she laughed, realizing she had just sounded exactly like her late grandmother.

Still, she was very careful to check the locks on all her doors when she left for work that morning.

4

EMILY WORRIED about going to work Monday morning. If Sam Jennings had been spreading his accusations around, as April had implied, Emily's co-workers might treat her differently, knowing she was a suspect in an embezzlement case. But if they'd heard, they gave no indication, though several wanted to question and tease her about the debacle at the baking contest.

They also wanted to ask her about her plans for the future, now that word had gotten out that she was selling her house. Emily answered their questions in vague terms, since she hadn't yet given notice that she would be leaving her job at the end of the year. And, whether her co-workers were aware of it or not, the investigation was still hanging over her head, along with her knowledge that she wouldn't be able to leave Honoria until it was settled.

The man who'd given her orders to stay in town called her at work that afternoon.

"What can I do for you, Chief Davenport?" she asked, keeping her voice low for privacy.

"There are a few more questions I'd like to ask you," he replied. "Do you have any free time after work this afternoon? Maybe we could talk over dinner."

Her pulse jumped. *Dinner?* Was he asking for an interview, or a date? She didn't know what made her more nervous.

"I'm afraid I can't meet you for dinner this evening," she said, keeping her tone light. "I have a meeting right after work. We'll be having finger sandwiches there."

"Maybe we could get together after your meeting. For coffee and dessert? You could answer my questions then."

Emily chewed her lower lip as she thought about it for a moment. And then she nodded. Might as well get this behind her. The sooner this case was cleared up, the sooner she would be free. "All right. Where?"

"Er—" He hesitated a moment, then said, "There's a sandwich and pie place just down the street from the police department. On Maple?"

"Yes, I know it." It wouldn't have been her first choice, but they were meeting to talk, not to eat, she reminded herself.

"What time can you be there?"

"Eight-thirty?"

"Fine. I'll see you then."

It wasn't a date, Emily reminded herself as she hung up the phone. Just an informal interview. So there was absolutely no reason for her to be looking forward to it with such anticipation.

WADE AND EMILY pulled up to the sandwich shop at almost the same moment. Climbing out of his Jeep, Wade nodded in greeting when Emily slipped out of her car.

"Evening, Ms. McBride," he said, trying to mask the full extent of his pleasure at seeing her again. Even after a day of work and her club meeting, she looked fresh and pretty in a royal blue pantsuit with a crisp white collar.

Though she looked as though she should be dining at an elegant restaurant rather than this second-rate sandwich shop, he thought, looking uncomfortably at the rather shabby facade. Maybe this place hadn't been such a great choice.

"Good evening, Chief Davenport." She waited for him to the join her at the entrance.

Wade reached around her to open the door, and caught a whiff of the faint, floral scent he already associated with her. "How was your meeting?" he asked as they entered the restaurant together.

"Just routine." She looked around the empty dining room, and Wade followed her glance. The tables were clean, though the floor could have used some work. A television set, bolted high on the wall in the back corner of the room, was still turned on, though no one was there to watch.

"I wonder if they're about to close," Emily murmured, indicating the empty tables.

Wade moved toward the order counter, which was unoccupied. The cash register sat at one end, apparently unguarded. Security was obviously not a priority for this business, he thought with a slight frown of disapproval. "Hello?"

In response to Wade's call, a skinny adolescent boy with shaggy, oily hair and an apparently permanent scowl wandered out from the kitchen. He stepped behind the order counter. "What'll y'all have?"

"We weren't sure you were still open," Wade said.

The teenager turned and yelled into the back. "What time are we closing tonight?"

"Nine o'clock. Same as every weeknight," an exasperated voice hollered back.

Wade glanced at Emily, noting that she was fighting a smile. "That should give us time for a quick bite. What would you like?"

She glanced at the menu displayed above the boy's head. "Pecan pie and coffee sounds good to me."

The boy scratched his chin, then turned again toward the door to the kitchen. "Hey, June? We got any coffee?" he bellowed.

"Billy Ray, you know the coffeemaker's been broken for a week," the unseen woman in the kitchen shouted irritably.

Billy Ray swiveled back to look glumly at Emily. "Ain't got no coffee."

Emily cleared her throat. "Then I'll just have an iced tea."

Nodding, Billy Ray turned to Wade. "What about you?"

"Ham and cheese on wheat."

"Lettuce and tomato?"

"Yes."

"Onion?"

Wade glanced at Emily. "No."

"Want something to drink with that?"

Wade was half tempted to ask for coffee, just to see if Billy Ray would remember that the coffeemaker was broken. Resisting the mischievous impulse, he said only, "Cola, please."

Billy Ray set their drinks on the counter, then nodded toward the empty dining room. "Sit down somewhere. I'll bring the food out when it's ready."

Inwardly groaning, Wade followed Emily to one of the dozen empty tables.

"A few of that boy's spark plugs aren't firing, I'm afraid," he murmured as they took their seats, using the noise of a deodorant commercial blaring from the television to mask his less-than-generous comment.

Emily giggled. "I'm afraid you're right. How do you suppose he knows when to go home if he doesn't know what time they close?"

"I guess whoever that is in the back just tells him to leave."

A loud screech from the television set caused both of them to look up—only to see a large, ugly insect engaged in battle with something even larger and uglier. An announcer's officious voice described the battle in gruesome detail, adding that the winner would feed the corpse of the loser to its offspring.

Emily's giggle turned into a laugh. "It's the nature channel. Oh, how appetizing."

The losing insect gave a dying squeal just as Billy Ray delivered the food to their table.

"Would you—um—mind turning the TV to another channel?" Wade asked, wondering if Billy Ray would have to yell for permission to do so.

But Billy Ray only shrugged and nodded. "Sure. We got cable."

He reached up, flipped the channel selector and walked away without waiting to see what he'd tuned in to.

Wade bit into his sandwich just as a hideous, slimy creature slashed a horrified space explorer's throat on the television screen. The poor guy gave a gurgling scream that echoed eerily in the nearly empty restaurant.

"I, um, think it's one of the *Alien* movies," Emily murmured when Wade choked on his sandwich.

Wade swallowed and then gave in to a chuckle as he pointedly turned his back to the television. "A real classy place I've brought you to, isn't it?"

Emily looked quickly down at her pie. "You said you have some questions to ask me, Chief Davenport?"

Wade almost winced. Emily had made it quite clear that she considered this nothing more than a business meeting, informal though it might be.

He reached into his shirt pocket and pulled out five slips of yellow paper. "Could you look at these for a moment, please?" he asked, keeping his tone neutral as he slid the papers across the table.

Emily picked them up, glanced at them for a moment, then fanned them on the table in front of her. "I initialed these two," she said, pointing with one pink-tipped finger. "Someone else wrote my initials on these three."

Wade nodded and slipped the papers back into his pocket. "Thanks."

After a moment, Emily frowned. "That's it? That's all you needed from me?"

"That's it for now. Thanks."

"Um—why didn't you just have me come by your office?"

He shrugged and took another bite of his sandwich, which tasted pretty good despite the restaurant's obvious shortcomings. After swallowing, he explained, "I didn't want you to be forced into any awkward explanations if anyone saw you being apparently interrogated in my office. And I knew I'd be hungry by this time. I'd seen this place a few times, and I thought it would be convenient for both of us, so..."

A fine cloud of dust drifted toward their table. On the other side of the room, Billy Ray wielded a broom with more vigor than skill.

Emily pushed the uneaten half of her pecan pie away. "I see. And now what?"

"Now I continue my investigation into Tammy Powell's whereabouts."

"I see." She clasped her hands in her lap. "Any idea how much longer this investigation might take?"

"No, but try to relax about it. I've found no evidence whatever linking you to this or any other crime. As I've told you before, I consider you a very unlikely suspect."

"Thank you," she murmured. "But I'm still forbidden to leave town until the investigation is over, right?"

He studied her thoughtfully, wondering again at her impatience to leave Honoria. And, once again, he found himself reluctant to see her go. "There's no reason you can't leave town for a few days, as long as you let me know where you're going, just as a formality. I have to at least make it look like I'm investigating you thoroughly, or Sam Jennings is likely to accuse me of incompetence. Again."

Emily scowled. "I don't have any plans to leave town for the moment, at least until after I've sold the house and made arrangements for my other things. But I don't like feeling as if I'm trapped here."

"And have you felt trapped here, Emily?" he asked, aware of the revealing undertones in her voice.

She looked down at her plate and nodded. "Sometimes," she murmured.

"It doesn't seem like such a bad place to be. With a few notable exceptions, the people of Honoria seem friendly and good-hearted. Crime's low, weather's nice, no traffic to speak of."

"I didn't say Honoria was a bad place," she reminded him, just a bit defensive now. "But I've lived here all my life. For the past five years or more, I've been unable to leave for more than a day or two at a time because there was no one to take care of my father. Now that he's gone, and nothing else is holding me here, this comes up. It just seems...unfair."

Feeling inexplicably contrite, Wade said, "I'm sorry."

"And the worst part is, I've never been the direct subject of gossip before. They talked about my mother and my brother and Savannah, but I've never done anything to bring attention to me. I still haven't, but my reputation is in danger of being trashed, anyway. I hate that."

"Emily, your reputation is not in danger of any kind. No one who really knows you will believe a word of this," Wade replied emphatically. "And I've warned Jennings again to keep his unsubstantiated suspicions to himself."

She looked up at him. "You, um, really don't think anyone who knows me would believe I'm guilty of this?"

If she was asking what *he* believed, Wade had no problem answering candidly. "No," he said. "I don't."

Her lower lip quivered, just a tiny bit, as if she'd been either touched or reassured by his words. Or both. Whatever the reason, it made Wade suddenly ravenously hungry...not for the rest of his sandwich, but for a taste of Emily.

She seemed to feel the need to fill the sudden taut silence between them with small talk. "How is Clay?"

Reining in his inappropriate emotions, Wade answered evenly. "Oh, he's doing great. He sure enjoyed that Ferris-wheel ride with you Saturday. Talked about it all afternoon. And he refused to wash his face before he went to bed that night. Didn't want to the next day, either, but since the paint had started to peel off by then, he finally agreed."

"I'm glad he had a good time. He's an adorable little boy."

"Thanks. I guess it's obvious that I'm pretty proud of him."

Wade was pleased to see Emily smile again. "Yes," she said. "That was obvious."

Shamelessly playing on her obvious soft spot for his kid, Wade boasted, "Did I mention how smart he is? He's got all *A*s in school. He's in third grade at Honoria Elementary."

"Who's his teacher?"

"Mrs. Flaherty."

Emily's smile widened. "Really? She was my third-grade teacher."

"You're kidding."

"I was in one of her first classes. She was my all-time favorite teacher."

"Clay's already very fond of her. I think she won

him over when he saw the *Star Wars* poster on her wall the first day of school."

"Clay likes *Star Wars*?"

"He's obsessed. Watches the videos over and over. Plays with all the action toys. He's dressing as Darth Vader for Halloween—again."

"Goldfish and aliens." Emily smiled. "You've got a cute kid, Chief."

"I know. Thanks. Would you like something else to drink?"

Emily glanced at the still-blaring television, and then at Billy Ray, who'd stopped sweeping to lean against his broom and stare slack jawed at the violent movie. "No, I think I've had enough, thank you."

Following the direction of her glance, Wade grinned. "Wouldn't want to overstrain poor Billy Ray, would we?"

"No. He looks exhausted, poor thing," Emily murmured, fighting a smile.

Wade pushed his chair back. "I'll walk you to your car."

"Are you off work now, or do you have to go back to the station?" Emily asked as they stepped outside.

"I have a few more things I need to do tonight. The good thing about working in a small town is that there's less crime to deal with. The bad thing is that there are fewer of us available to take care of what we've got—like those break-ins that happened during the festival Saturday. I took a couple of hours off earlier to spend some time with Clay, then headed back to work after the housekeeper put him to bed at eight."

"Oh, you have a housekeeper?"

Wade nodded. "Cecilia Sanchez. She's our live-in housekeeper, nanny, cook and friend."

Emily paused beside her car, turning to look at Wade. "She came with you from Atlanta?"

"Yeah. She's been with us almost five years. Since Clay's mother died," he added.

He noted the look of distress that flashed across Emily's face. "I'm sorry," she said. "I'd been told that you were widowed, but I didn't realize that Clay was so very young when he lost his mother."

He nodded, uncomfortable with her expression of sympathy. "I talked to Mary Kay again about your place yesterday," he said, abruptly changing the subject. "Has she called you yet to set up an appointment?"

"I haven't been home. She probably left a message on my answering machine, so I'll call her to arrange something."

"You—uh—still haven't made any plans for after you sell your house? Once everything else is settled and you're free to leave, that is?"

"No. I'm just ready to try something new. I know it's an old cliché, but I guess I'm ready to go 'find myself.'" She smiled wryly.

Wade didn't wince, but he had to make an effort not to. He'd heard words to that effect before...from his wife. With disastrous results all around.

Hearing the same thing from Emily made him realize that asking her out—as he had fully intended to do before this evening ended—was probably not such a good idea. He no longer wanted to pursue relationships that would lead nowhere. Emily would obviously have no interest in a man whose only desire now was to settle into a comfortable home with his son in sleepy little Honoria.

"It isn't always necessary to go someplace new to find yourself," he couldn't resist pointing out. "Happiness isn't a place, you know. It's a state of mind."

"Yes, I know," she said, but with a breeziness that left Wade wondering if she really believed him. "But I'm still looking forward to seeing places I've only read about until now."

"I hope you'll find what you're looking for," he said, and he meant that sincerely. He genuinely liked Emily McBride. He wanted her to be happy—even though he wasn't sure that she would be in the footloose life she'd fantasized.

"Thank you," she said, and smiled.

That smile made him reconsider his decision not to ask her out. Okay, so maybe she was only going to be around for a couple more months. There was no reason they couldn't spend a few pleasant evenings together, was there? He didn't have to do anything stupid like fall in love with her, did he?

A beat-up old car sped past with a squeal of tires. Wade looked after it with a frown, making note of the license tag. "That O'Brien boy is speeding again. I can see I'm going to have to step up traffic patrol," he murmured. "The teenagers around here like to drive just a little too fast—especially that one."

Emily's expression turned rueful. "They claim that fast driving is the most excitement to be had around here."

"Sounds like maybe you agree with them."

She shook her head. "I don't believe in endangering

lives by driving recklessly. But I do understand that kids get bored. There really isn't much for them to do."

"Someone should consider starting some after-school programs for teens. But in the meantime, they're going to have to learn that traffic rules will be enforced in this town while I'm on watch."

Emily laughed. "You sound just like a cop."

He couldn't resist reaching out to touch her, though he contented himself with teasing the ends of her golden curls. "I *am* a cop."

He didn't think he was imagining the awareness in her eyes when she looked at him. Emily didn't see him only as a cop, any more than he had ever thought of her as nothing more than a suspect.

Her smile died when he continued to gaze down at her, standing so close that their bodies were almost touching. All he would have to do was lean forward a couple of inches, and her mouth would be close enough for him to take that taste he'd been craving all evening.

He wasn't holding her there—she could easily take a step backward if she felt uncomfortable. But she didn't immediately move away, which gave him courage.

"This wasn't much of a dinner," he said, jerking his chin toward the restaurant. He could see Billy Ray through the window, still leaning on his broom and watching television. "I'd like to take you someplace a little nicer next time. How about it?"

Emily's left eyebrow rose a fraction of an inch. "Are you asking me for a date?"

"Yeah. My social skills have gotten a little rusty, but that's what I'm trying to do. Would you like to have dinner with me sometime?"

She hesitated, then stepped back.

"Thank you, but I'm afraid I have very little free time right now," she said, avoiding his eyes. "I have a lot of work to do, preparing for the move, so many details to finalize. I think I'd better concentrate on getting that stuff done for now. And as long as your investigation is ongoing, it's probably best for us not to socialize. Isn't that right?"

Okay, she'd made her feelings clear enough. She wasn't interested. She'd tried to be nice about it, though, so Wade managed a smile that he hoped looked somewhat genuine. "Yes, I suppose so. And, having just been through a big move myself, I know how much time and work is involved."

Emily's smile held a touch of relief—and maybe just a little regret? Or was that only wishful thinking on Wade's part?

"Yes, well, thank you for the coffee and pie, Chief, er, Wade. I'll be seeing you around."

"Sure. Good night, Emily. Drive carefully."

She nodded and climbed into her car.

Wade felt himself scowling as he headed toward his Jeep after Emily drove away. Moping like a kid who'd been turned down for the prom. And he hoped he wasn't foolish enough to fall for a woman who could very well prove to be another heartbreaker.

One thing was for sure. He was spending entirely too much time thinking about Emily McBride.

OLIVER WAS DANCING impatiently by the time Emily got home. She'd made a quick trip during her lunch hour to let him out, but he was ready to go again.

"I will be so glad when your owners get home," she

told him, holding the door so that he could waddle quickly outside. "You're entirely too much responsibility. Their cruise should have ended today, so they'll be home by Wednesday. Two more days and you're out of here, buddy."

Oliver didn't seem offended at her impatience to be rid of him. He sniffed around the yard in the darkness, taking his time now despite his earlier haste. Emily sat on the edge of the porch and kept a close eye on him, using the bright moonlight for illumination. Night creatures serenaded her from the woods. It was a lovely and peaceful scene. And so lonely that Emily's heart ached.

It wasn't that she'd been particularly close to her father. Josiah McBride, Jr. had not allowed anyone to be close to him, including his only daughter. But since his death, Emily had been even more aware of how alone she was. And how little she'd actually done with her life.

Something rustled in the trees near the driveway and Oliver barked.

"Quiet, Oliver," Emily said. "It's probably just a deer. The woods are full of them."

Oliver posed threateningly for a few more moments, then lost interest in the now quiet trees and went back to his search for the perfect spot to do his business.

"Sometime tonight would be nice," Emily prodded him impatiently. "I have things to do, you know."

Oliver snorted as if in disbelief that she had anything more important to attend to than him.

Emily glared at him. "Stupid dog. Despite whatever conclusions you might have drawn during the past few days, I do have a life."

That statement reminded her of the rather lame excuses she'd made when Wade Davenport had asked her out.

She hadn't exactly been surprised that he'd wanted to spend some time with her. And it hadn't been easy for her to decline. She liked him. Maybe she could have gone out with him once or twice, as long as they both knew that casual dating was all it would be. After all, she'd made it clear to him that she wouldn't be around much longer, that she had places to go, things to do. Settling down in her lifelong hometown with a ready-made family was not a part of her plans—even if Wade was thinking along those lines, which he probably was not.

But something had made her turn him down. Maybe it had been instinct, or perhaps just overdeveloped caution, but her responses to Wade Davenport had warned her that it wouldn't be easy to date him casually. He was a man who could tempt her to forget her lofty plans, and to start indulging in foolish daydreams that were liable to get her hurt.

She wondered if Wade still grieved for his wife. If he'd been deeply, passionately in love with his son's mother. Did Wade simply want someone to substitute for his first wife and be a mother to Clay?

And then she wondered why she was wondering about things like that—hadn't she just told herself that Wade's future was none of her business, since she wouldn't be around to see it?

She thought of Wade's interest in her house. He would be the first potential buyer to look at it. Maybe he would buy it. She tried to imagine him living here with Clay. Something about that image felt right. She could so clearly picture little Clay running through the same woods she had played in as a child. She could almost see Wade puttering around in the yard, nailing new boards onto the porch, mowing the grass in the summertime.

That thought intrigued her. She entertained herself for a moment by imagining Wade pushing a lawnmower on a hot summer afternoon. The bright Georgia sun would bring out the red highlights in his glossy brown hair. Maybe he would take off his shirt. She imagined muscles moving beneath his skin, sweat glistening on his back and biceps.

Expanding the fantasy, she pictured little Clay running across the freshly mowed grass, maybe chasing a puppy. And a woman standing on the porch, just about where she was now sitting. In fact, the woman in the fantasy looked a lot like herself....

Oliver barked again, bringing Emily sharply out of the daydream. Appalled at the direction her thoughts had taken, she scowled and shook her head, driving the lingering mental pictures away. What on earth was she doing? Maybe Wade Davenport would buy this house, and maybe he and little Clay would settle down here with someone—but it certainly wouldn't be Emily.

She would be off having adventures. She would be meeting people who had never heard of the McBrides, who wouldn't look at her and see Nadine's daughter or Lucas's sister. She would be finding out who she was and what she really wanted out of life. Chasing those dreams she'd written about in the letter she'd once buried in a makeshift time capsule.

For the first time in her life, Emily wanted to be truly

selfish. To take care of no one but herself. And she told herself that she couldn't wait to begin—even if the thought of leaving her home left an oddly hollow feeling inside her.

5

IT WAS EARLY Wednesday evening, two days after her meeting with Wade, when Emily's phone rang with yet another request for her time.

"Come on, Emily, please. We really need your help," Tressie Bearden pleaded. "Don't turn us down."

Emily swallowed a groan. "Tressie, I really don't have time for this. Why in the world did you wait until the second week of October to start planning a Halloween haunted house? You should have begun weeks ago."

"I know, I know. But our club heard that the Jaycees were going to do one, and we've just found out that their plans fell through, so no one's putting one on this year. We thought we could throw one together real quick and maybe make a few dollars for next year's projects, you know? But none of us on the fund-raising committee have ever done a haunted house before and we know you've been involved with them before with other groups, and we knew you'd help if we asked. Say you will, Emily. You know how much our club needs the money for our projects. Think of all the Christmas toys we can buy for the needy children."

Low blow, Emily thought with a wince. Tressie knew Toys for Toddlers was one of Emily's pet projects.

"But, Tressie, a haunted house is very difficult to organize. It requires a lot of planning, manpower and expense. You could end up losing money if you don't pull it all together."

"We've got lots of people who said they would help," Tressie countered eagerly. "All we need is someone to help us get started. And since you've got experience..."

Emily could have said no. She even opened her mouth to do so. And then she thought of the toddlers who would get a few extra toys because of this project. And she realized that it might be the last time she could help raise money for the needy children of Honoria.

"All right, Tressie," she said. "I'll come to your meeting tomorrow night to talk about it. But no promises until we see where we stand, all right?"

"Great!" Emily's old schoolmate sounded exultant—and totally oblivious to Emily's hesitation. "I told everyone you would do it. I knew you wouldn't let us down."

"We'll talk about it at the meeting."

"Sure. This is going to be so much fun."

Tressie hung up before Emily could tell her that running a haunted house fund-raiser was much more work than fun.

"I'm only doing this because I want to," Emily said out loud as she hung up the phone. "Not because I'm a doormat who can't say no."

Her voice sounded oddly skeptical as it echoed through the empty room.

Her phone rang again only a few minutes later. Wondering what they wanted from her *now*, Emily answered it warily.

To her relief, it was her aunt, who had just called to chat. "Everyone's talking about you selling the house," she said after a few minutes. "They all want to know what your plans are. Marvella asked if you were moving into one of those new apartments over on Magnolia Street. I told her I wasn't sure what you were planning."

"Thanks. It's really no one's business yet. I thought I'd leave Honoria and just travel for awhile."

Bobbie's sigh echoed clearly through the telephone lines. "You sound just like my three children," she complained. "Not one of them wanted to settle here. Trevor's off in Washington and Trent's at the Air Force Academy, and now Tara's marrying that private investigator and plans to live permanently in Atlanta. You're the last of your generation still here, and now you want to leave. None of you young people think our little hometown has enough to offer."

Emily saw no need to mention how much she'd envied her cousins, who'd had the courage and the freedom to chase their dreams. Now Savannah and Tara were both deliriously in love with interesting and exciting men, Trevor was happily married and the father of an adorable son, and Trent was flying jet planes, preparing for a life of adventure.

Lucas...well, Emily didn't know where her half brother had gone, but he hadn't stayed around to be the object of gossip. She would never understand why he hadn't told her goodbye, or why he'd never contacted her again after he left, but she had never really blamed him for leaving. Even if it had meant that Emily's life had to be put on hold while their father had been unable to take care of himself.

But understanding her brother's actions hadn't stopped Emily from missing him. Or wishing she'd had the freedom to follow his example. Now she did. And she was going to let nothing—or no one—stand in her way.

"I was rather hoping," Bobbie said, "that you and that nice young police chief would hit it off. You seemed so friendly at the fall festival."

Emily gulped. "I—um—"

"He's a widower, you know. And a very attractive man, don't you think?"

"Well, yes, but—"

"I was thinking about inviting you both over for dinner. Wouldn't you like to get to know him a little better, Emily? He could be Mr. Right."

But Emily wasn't looking for Mr. Right. Especially when the nearest candidate was a man who intended to settle permanently in Honoria. A man who came with a young son and all the responsibilities that accompanied a ready-made family.

"No, please, Aunt Bobbie. Don't start matchmaking. I'm really not interested just now, okay?"

Bobbie wasn't pleased that her romantic plotting had been derailed and she made little effort to hide it. But she seemed to realize she could hardly force her niece into a courtship. "All right, Emily, if that's what you want."

"Thank you."

"Come for Sunday lunch after church." Bobbie spoke with the imperious air developed through many years of teaching junior-high-school students.

Though it was more of a command than an invitation, Emily accepted graciously. "All right. Thank you, I'd love to join you and Uncle Caleb for Sunday lunch."

Emily hung up with a weary sigh. She hoped her aunt would just leave well enough alone. As kind-hearted as she was, Aunt Bobbie could be ruthless when she set herself a goal.

Emily had set a goal of her own—to get out of Honoria. To find the dreams she'd somehow lost during the past few years.

And she wasn't going to let her loyalty to her family or her attraction to Honoria's new police chief stand in the way.

CONSIDERING THE WAY things had been going, Emily shouldn't have been surprised that Wade Davenport was the first person she saw at the Honoria Community League Thursday evening. Maybe if she *had* prepared herself, she wouldn't have reacted to the sight of him with a racing pulse, a catch in her throat, and a blush on her cheeks.

Emily could only hope that no one noticed.

"Hello, Wade," she said, greeting him casually. "Have you become a member of the Community League?"

"Actually, I'm just visiting tonight. I had several invitations, and I thought it would be a good way to meet a few locals I haven't gotten to know yet," he explained.

She nodded. "Good idea. I hope there will be a nice attendance this evening. The club's membership has been dropping during the past few years. People seem to be too busy at home to get involved in community-service organizations."

"You seem to stay very active in the community."

She made a face. "I have a speech impediment. Can't seem to say that two-letter word that begins with *n* and ends with *o*."

Wade laughed. "I've suffered from that same malady at times. It's a real pain to have a social conscience, isn't it?"

"Chief Davenport! I'm so glad you could make it tonight." Leslie Anne Cantrell bore down on them with a beaming smile and a not-so-subtle wiggle in her walk. "Come in and let me introduce you to everyone. Oh, hi, Emily," she added offhandedly, already towing Wade away.

Apparently, Emily thought dryly, Leslie Anne had set her sights on yet another single man. She'd already been through most of Honoria's eligible bachelors—and a few that hadn't been technically eligible. Every town had at least one man-eater, and Leslie Anne was Honoria's—now that Emily's mother was no longer around.

Emily briefly considered warning Wade about the woman—and then she shook her head, telling herself not to be silly. Wade Davenport was certainly capable of taking care of himself where women were concerned. And it was none of Emily's business, anyway.

She was acting as if she was jealous that Leslie Anne had practically draped herself all over Wade. And that, of course, was ridiculous. Emily had no reason at all to be jealous over Wade Davenport.

WADE WATCHED Emily during the meeting. He tried to be discreet about it, but he couldn't seem to keep his eyes from turning her direction. She looked so pretty in a soft, pale green sweater that seemed designed for touching. Though he'd attempted to put her out of his mind since their meeting at the sandwich shop, he hadn't been particularly successful.

Seeing her this evening—and reacting to her as he did—reminded him why.

He winced a little as he thought of her joke that she was unable to say "no." She'd had no problem doing so with him. But he could see how much trouble she had resisting the club members, who seemed determined to make her chairwoman of their put-together-at-the-last-possible-minute haunted-house project. By the time the meeting ended, Emily had managed to refuse that position, but still agreed to help. Wade suspected that she would be doing most of the work, since few others in the group of approximately thirty people seemed to have any trouble making excuses.

It occurred to him that nearly every time he'd seen her, she'd been doing something for others. Dogsitting. Painting faces and judging a baking contest. Taking his son on a Ferris-wheel ride. Helping with this project. Since he'd been seen with her at the festival, several people had described her to him as a young woman with a big heart and an overdeveloped social conscience.

While Wade admired her generosity, he wondered how much of it had been influenced by the unhappy family history he'd heard about. Deserted at a very young age by her mother. Later abandoned by her older brother. Left alone to care for her father during his lengthy illness. Had she become a "people pleaser" because of that background?

He thought of her rather vague plans to leave Honoria, to find a life for herself somewhere else. He supposed he could understand that she would be ready to stop living for everyone else and start taking care of Emily. He even understood the urge to get away from what she knew and try to find happiness somewhere else. After all, hadn't that been exactly what he'd been doing when he'd left the bustle of Atlanta for quiet little Honoria?

He couldn't help wondering, though, if Emily would find out the hard way that real peace came from within, not from outward surroundings. It was a lesson Wade himself was still trying to learn.

"So, do you think you can help us out any with the haunted house, Chief Davenport?" The man who asked was thin, except for a slight pudge above his belt, and had a premature bald spot developing at the back of his head. Wade thought his name was Arnie something-or-other, and that he owned a small convenience store at the west end of Main Street.

"I don't have much spare time to commit to the project," Wade answered, unwilling to sacrifice any more of the hours he was able to spend with his son. "But I'll make sure you have plenty of security for the event. Sometimes crowds get out of hand at this sort of attraction."

His promise apparently satisfied the members of the club, who all nodded contentedly. Wade could tell they didn't expect any real trouble with their project. Any group that put together a haunted house in Atlanta would have considered security one of the first priorities, he thought with a slight smile.

Wade managed to find a place by the door so that he just happened to be in a position to walk Emily to her car. Even as he fell into step beside her, he felt uncomfortably like a teenager hanging around the locker of the cheerleader he had a crush on, hoping she would notice him. Pushing that sheepish analogy to the back of his mind, he cleared his throat.

"Interesting meeting."

Emily groaned softly and glanced around to make sure no one could hear her. "I can't believe they think they're going to pull all this together in less than three weeks."

"You don't think it can be done?"

"Oh, sure, it can be done. If someone is willing to work her fingers off."

Her dry tone let Wade know exactly who Emily expected to be doing all that work. "You could have always said no," he suggested.

She smiled wryly and shook her head. "You're forgetting about my speech impediment. That word just won't seem to come out of my mouth—especially when others hint that there will be no toys for toddlers this Christmas if I don't help with this project."

"Sucker."

She chuckled in response to his teasing tone. "That's me."

"You have a kind heart, Emily McBride," he said, sobering. "That's nothing to apologize for."

He thought she might have blushed a little, though it was hard to tell in the artificial lighting of the parking lot. She changed the subject. "I understand you're coming to look at my house Saturday morning with your Realtor."

"Yes. She assured me that would be a convenient time for you."

"Of course." They had reached her car. Emily slid her key into the lock and glanced at Wade over her shoulder. "Well...good night, Wade."

The security lamp above and behind him illuminated her face, highlighting her blond curls, gleaming softly in her blue eyes, making her mouth glisten.

Her mouth. Wade found himself staring at her lips, at the tiny dimple at the right corner, imagining the feel and taste of her.

He wanted to kiss her. Wanted it so badly that he felt a fine tremor run through him as he worked to resist the urge.

Damn. What was happening here? When was the last time any woman had made his hands shake?

He shoved them quickly into his pockets, and out of danger.

He reminded himself that they weren't on a date. That Emily had made it clear that she wasn't interested in dating him. But that didn't change the fact that he still wanted to kiss her.

He realized that he was still staring at her mouth. He quickly lifted his gaze, only to find his eyes locked with hers. And his mind emptied of coherent thought.

"Wade?" Emily sounded uncertain. "Good night."

"Oh. Uh, yeah. See you around."

He forced himself to take a step backward. It was probably the hardest step he'd ever taken.

After a moment, Emily climbed into her car and closed the door with a decisive snap. Wade walked to his Jeep, cursing himself for acting like an idiot around this woman. For wanting something he couldn't have. And for proving, once again, that he had a real knack for being attracted to women who were entirely wrong for him.

HE HAD WANTED to kiss her.

As she drove home with that thought echoing in her mind, Emily tried to tell herself that she was being silly. Fanciful. Conceited. Wade had done absolutely nothing to indicate that he wanted to kiss her. Except to look at her mouth. For what had seemed like a very long time. And then he'd met her eyes with what might have been a glint of hunger in his.

She shook her head, muttering to herself. Apparently, it wasn't enough that she had developed this embarrassingly juvenile and ill-timed crush on Honoria's new chief of police. Now she was trying to convince herself that he felt the same way about her.

Ridiculous.

And even if he was attracted to her—if only a little— she'd already decided that it would be unwise to act on that attraction. Especially considering that she was still officially a suspect in his case. And now that she'd gotten reluctantly involved in a project that was going to take most of her free time for the rest of the month, she simply didn't have time to get involved in a relationship, or an affair, or whatever it was that Wade Davenport might have had in mind when he'd looked at her and thought about kissing her.

WADE DROVE UP to Emily's house Saturday morning and noted immediately that his Realtor's car wasn't there. Though he was on time—it was exactly ten o'clock—apparently he'd beaten her there. He wondered if he should wait in the car for her to arrive, or get out and ring Emily's doorbell.

Clay settled the question for him. He had his door open and was out of the car the moment Wade turned off the engine.

"Daddy, I *like* this house," said the child who'd found something to criticize about both of the houses they'd visited before. Wade hadn't even told him who owned this one.

Wade climbed out of the Jeep. "What do you like about it?"

Hands on his slender hips, Clay cocked his red head and looked thoughtfully around. "I like the porch. And the big trees. And the...Daddy, look! It's Miss Emily."

Wade swiveled around to find Emily watching them from her porch. And despite all the lectures he'd given himself on the way over about acting like an adult and responding to her with his brains instead of his libido, he still had to gulp before he could force a smile.

He still wanted to kiss her.

"Good morning," he said. "Are we early?"

"No. Actually, there's a slight problem. Mary Kay just called. Her husband has been rushed to the hospital for emergency surgery and she's going to have to break your appointment this morning."

"That's terrible. I hope he'll be all right."

"She seemed to think everything will be okay once the operation is over. An appendectomy, I think."

"We'll reschedule, then."

Emily shook her head. "You're here now. Why don't I show you the place?"

"This is your house, Miss Emily?" Clay asked, wide-eyed.

Emily smiled. "Yes. Would you like to see it, Clay?"

He nodded fervently and skipped toward the porch where she stood. "Yes, please."

Wade followed more sedately, wondering if this was such a good idea, after all. It seemed that a weakness for Emily McBride was something the Davenport men shared. Clay was gazing at her like a lovesick puppy— and Wade could only hope that he wasn't wearing a similar expression.

Emily held out her hand to Clay, who promptly slipped his into it. "Come on," she said, glancing back at Wade. "I'll show you around."

Wade had already seen the living room, of course, though Emily paused there to give him a chance to look it over again. Clay headed straight for the table that held all the framed photographs. "Who are all these people?" he asked.

"Clay, we're here to see the house, not Miss Emily's personal things," Wade reminded his son.

Emily ignored him. "Those are all photographs of members of my family," she explained to Clay. "The oldest picture is of my grandparents, Josiah and Anna Mae McBride. The others are all photos of their descendents."

"What are descendents?" The boy stumbled a little over the word.

"People who have descended from them—their children and grandchildren," Emily explained patiently. "These are all pictures of my aunts, uncles, cousins, my parents and my brother."

Giggling, Clay pointed to the photograph of the Irish setter that Wade had noticed on his last visit. "Is that a descendent, too?" the child asked impishly.

"No," Emily answered with a smile. "That was my dog, Reilly. He was the smartest dog in the world."

"What happened to him?"

"He died a few years ago. He was very old."

Clay gazed soulfully up at Emily. "Do you miss him?"

Wade noted a touch of sadness in Emily's eyes when she nodded. "Yes. I still miss him sometimes. But I had a wonderful time with him while I had him."

Was it loneliness that Emily was running from by selling her house? Wade couldn't stop trying to understand an action that just didn't seem to fit the woman he was slowly coming to know.

Still holding Clay's hand, Emily took them through the kitchen—which, as Wade had suspected, was large and well-appointed but in need of some general maintenance. Then they looked into a formal dining room with fading wallpaper. At the back of the house were four bedrooms, three furnished as bedrooms, one as a home office. The last bedroom they entered was obviously Emily's own. Done in dark greens and maroons, it had a cozy, lived-in look. *A retreat*, Wade thought. *A sanctuary*.

It wasn't the master bedroom. She'd already shown him that one, which was larger, and furnished in a masculine style that suggested it had been her father's room, though it had apparently been stripped of any personal effects after his death. Emily's room was probably the smallest of the three bedrooms. But it had the largest windows, which she'd filled with healthy houseplants.

"Is this where you sleep?" Clay wanted to know.

"Yes, this is my room," Emily confirmed, avoiding Wade's eyes.

"Is this where you'll sleep if my daddy and me move in?"

Wade took pity on her, stepping in before she was forced to explain. "If we buy Miss Emily's house, she will move out," he told his son.

Clay frowned. "You don't have to do that," he said. "You can stay, can't she, Daddy?"

This time it was Wade who groped for words, "Er—"

"I have fresh pastries in the kitchen," Emily said quickly. "Would you like a snack, Clay? And there's coffee if you'd like some, Wade, before we go outside to look around."

"Sounds good," Wade agreed, seizing the excuse. "Clay? Are you hungry?"

"I'm always hungry," Clay said with a matter-of-factness that brought Emily's smile back.

As the three of them headed back to the kitchen, Wade thought of Clay's innocent question. And he tried to block out the images of Emily living here with them—though not necessarily sleeping in her own room.

6

CLAY TOOK ONE LOOK at the old tire swing hanging from a massive oak branch in Emily's backyard, and he was gone, sprinting toward the tree with the enthusiastic determination of childhood.

"It's safe," Emily assured Wade. "I have the rope checked frequently, since my youngest visitors always love to play on that swing."

"Fresh-baked cookies and a tire swing in a big backyard," Wade murmured with a smile. "I bet you get a lot of young visitors."

She saw no need to tell him how often she was asked to baby-sit. Since her married friends with young children generally expected Emily to be home on weekends, they didn't hesitate to call. Even when her father had been alive, they had asked—after all, Josiah had been confined to his bed for years and hadn't kept Emily so busy that she couldn't keep an eye on a few children. Unless her father had been having one of his difficult days, Emily had usually said yes. She loved children. And she rarely had other plans.

To Wade, she said only, "I enjoy having children visit."

Dividing his attention between his son and the property, Wade looked around, examining the house's foundation, siding, gutters, roofing. Emily doubted that he missed anything, from the basic soundness of the place to the work that needed to be done. Work she'd neglected during the past year, when her father's medical bills had piled up and his care had grown more demanding. Since his death, she'd done only the general maintenance required to get the house ready to sell.

Wade asked questions about the property lines, about wildlife that lived in the woods surrounding the yard, about the insurance rates and fire-protection services. All the questions anybody else interested in the house would ask. But even as Emily answered them, she suspected his mind was already made up.

Something told her that her first potential buyer was the one who would end up with the place. Assuming they could come to an agreement on price—and she would leave that to the Realtor, for the most part— Wade would probably be living here next year. Again, she had that funny, hollow feeling at the thought of someone else in her house, cooking in her kitchen, working in her yard.

Emily had never lived anywhere except in this house. The thought of moving out was as unnerving as it was intriguing.

But this was what she wanted to do, she reminded herself. She had no intention of spending the rest of her life in this one house, following the same routines, seeing the same faces, never having experienced any of the world outside the confines of Honoria, Georgia.

The real Emily McBride was out there somewhere, and she was going to find her.

Finally tiring of the swing, Clay ran toward them. Wade caught his son and lifted him high in the air, causing the boy to squeal and giggle. The bond between Wade and Clay was so strong that Emily could almost see it.

She watched them wistfully, reminded that she'd never had that relationship with her own father, who'd become hardened and embittered long before she was old enough to understand. Her half brother, the product of Josiah's first marriage, had never gotten along well with their father. Emily had always suspected that he'd left town as much to escape his father's constant criticism and disapproval as the rumors that had spread about him.

Wade set Clay on his feet, then turned to Emily with one hand still resting on his son's shoulder. "Thank you for showing us around," he said.

"You're welcome. Would you like another cup of coffee before you go?"

"No, thank you. I promised Clay we'd have lunch and then take in a movie this afternoon. Would you like to join us?"

The invitation seemed spur-of-the-moment. Clay immediately seconded it, looking so sincere that it warmed Emily's heart. She came very close to saying yes. The word hovered on the tip of her tongue for a long moment.

But then she shook her head. "Thank you, but I can't. I have plans for the afternoon."

The plans weren't anything that couldn't be postponed for a few hours, but Emily stuck to her excuse. She already found both Clay and his father dangerously appealing. It seemed to her that she would only be flirting with disaster if she got further involved with either one of them at this point.

Clay looked disappointed. If Wade felt a similar emotion, he hid it well. He merely nodded and said, "Thanks again for the tour. I'll be in touch."

Clay hugged Emily before they left. "'Bye, Miss Emily."

"'Bye, Clay. Enjoy your movie."

She watched them drive away with a wistfulness that made her wonder if she should have accepted their invitation, after all. And then she shook her head, thought again of her goals, and turned to walk back into her empty house. It would be her house for only a brief time longer, she reminded herself. And that was exactly the way she wanted it...right?

WHAT EMILY HADN'T considered when she'd made up her mind to resist Wade Davenport's charms was the possibility that others, having concluded that she and Wade made a nice couple, would conspire to bring them together.

When Emily arrived at her aunt and uncle's house for Sunday lunch, she found Wade and Clay already there.

"You remember Chief Davenport, don't you, Emily?" her aunt Bobbie asked with an exaggeratedly innocent smile.

Emily gave her aunt a look that promised a long, serious conversation later, then forced a smile. "Of course."

Clay threw his arms around Emily's waist. "Hi, Miss Emily."

Very aware of her aunt's approving gaze, Emily returned the hug warmly. "Hi, Clay. I really like that shirt you're wearing."

Clay preened in his long-sleeved black T-shirt with a picture of Darth Vadar on the front. "It's new," he said. "My daddy got it for me."

"I didn't, however, expect him to insist on wearing it to church and Sunday lunch," Wade murmured. "I tried to talk him into something else, but he had his heart set on wearing this one, and it didn't seem worth the battle to change his mind."

"I think he looks just fine," Emily assured him with a smile.

"Could have been worse, I guess. He could have wanted a tattoo."

Emily laughed.

Looking quite pleased with herself, Bobbie waved to Emily from across the room. "Come say hello to your uncle."

Emily gave Wade a rather rueful smile. "She's been a schoolteacher for more than thirty years," she whispered. "She just can't stop talking like one, even at home."

Nevertheless, she moved obediently to kiss her uncle's lined cheek. "Hello, Uncle Caleb. How's your arm?"

He smiled fondly at her and flexed his left arm, which he'd injured in a fall at the golf course a few weeks earlier. "Much better, thank you, dear. Doc Horton says it'll be as good as new in another couple of weeks."

"I'm glad to hear it."

"Have you had any nibbles on your house yet?"

Emily looked involuntarily across the room to where Wade stood chatting with Bobbie and Marvella

Tucker, a longtime neighbor of the senior McBrides. "One or two," she replied vaguely.

Caleb followed her glance. "I hear Chief Davenport's interested."

Emily should have known that her uncle, the small town's longest practicing attorney, would have already heard the gossip. "He's looked at the house," she admitted.

"Don't you let him pay too little for the place, you hear? That property's worth a good bit. The house could use some work, but it's still sound. You deserve a fair market price for it."

Emily nodded. "I'll bring any offers to you, Uncle Caleb. I always value your advice."

Her uncle beamed. He'd been Emily's advisor on legal and personal matters for a very long time, something her own father, Caleb's older brother, had never been even before his illness had robbed him of his ability to communicate. Emily was fond of all her family, but she had a special place in her heart for her uncle Caleb.

The doorbell chimed. "That'll be Brother Tatum and Jennie," Bobbie said. "I'll go let them in, and then we'll be ready to eat."

Of course Bobbie had invited the minister on one of the few Sundays Emily had chosen to be lazy and sleep in. She sighed, knowing she would be in for delicate questioning from the minister's wife, who took a rather maternal attitude toward her husband's flock.

This could prove to be a very long afternoon.

Officious as always, Bobbie ushered everyone into the dining room and directed the seating. Emily doubted it was coincidence that she ended up seated at

Wade's left, with Clay at Wade's right. Caleb and Brother Tatum took the head and foot of the table, respectively, leaving Bobbie, Marvella Tucker and the minister's wife opposite Emily.

Very cozy.

Emily glanced at Wade to find him watching her with a gleam of amusement in his warm brown eyes. She suspected he'd guessed that Bobbie was trying her hand at matchmaking. If it bothered him, he didn't let it show. Outwardly, he seemed perfectly comfortable.

She suspected that Wade was quite proficient at concealing his true feelings. That stolid, laid-back manner of his had caused Martha Godwin to doubt his intelligence. Emily had never underestimated him so naively.

The three older women made sure that conversation did not lag during the meal. Wade and Emily answered when spoken to, and contributed when expected. Young Clay, exhibiting excellent table manners, said little, though Emily got the impression he didn't miss much.

Again, she had the feeling that Clay was unusually mature in some ways. She wondered if it was because he'd lost his mother so early—a bond Emily shared with the boy. She wished she were sitting next to him so they could talk. She wasn't quite as comfortable chatting with Wade when she knew that every adult at the table was watching them with varying degrees of interest.

"This ham is simply delicious, Bobbie. Best I've had in years," Jennie Tatum, the minister's plump wife, pronounced as she enthusiastically attacked her meal. "What is your secret?"

Bobbie looked delighted by the praise. "Thank you, Jennie. I cooked it the way my mother always did—basted in Coca-Cola."

"These sweet potatoes with pecan topping are great," Wade chipped in. "How do you stay so trim, Caleb, married to such a good cook?"

"Golf and fishing," Caleb replied. "You play golf, Wade?"

"Badly."

"He fishes," Clay announced. "Once he caught a great big fish that he stuck on a board and hung on the wall."

The adults all smiled indulgently at the child.

"Getting close to the height of deer season," Caleb went on. "You do any deer hunting, Wade?"

"Some. But I have to admit, I prefer fishing."

"Squirrel. Now that's good eating," eighty-year-old Marvella Tucker mused aloud, looking up from her rapidly emptying plate. "My mama used to make the best squirrel and dumplin's ever. Her dumplin's were so light they near floated off'n the plate. You ever hunt any squirrel, boy?"

Wade and Clay looked at each other, trying to decide which one of them she had addressed. Wade finally seemed to conclude that she was talking to him—correctly, Emily thought with a stifled smile. To Marvella, anyone under fifty was a boy.

"Yes, ma'am, I've done some squirrel hunting in my time. I used to hunt with my dad when I was a boy back in Alabama. But, as I said, I prefer fishing these days."

Marvella turned her attention back to her meal.

"Are your parents still living, Chief Davenport?" Bobbie inquired.

"Call me Wade," he suggested. "And no, they're both gone now. I lost my father when I was twenty and my mother passed away a couple of years ago."

His wife and both his parents. Wade had suffered many losses in the past few years, Emily mused, feeling that they had even more in common than she'd originally believed.

Bobbie wasn't finished with her less-than-subtle interrogation. "Do you have any siblings, Wade?"

"A sister, Pamela. She and her husband live near Birmingham with their three kids."

"You going to ask him his social-security number next, Bobbie? Let the boy eat."

Marvella's dry interjection caused Caleb to laugh aloud, while the others struggled against smiles. Bobbie looked torn between being amused and offended. Amusement won out.

"I didn't mean to pry," she assured Wade. "I just like to get to know people."

He nodded. "No offense was taken, Mrs. McBride."

"Bobbie," she corrected him.

Emily was all too aware of how closely Wade was sitting to her. She was right-handed, he left-handed, so their arms occasionally bumped. Though Wade murmured a polite apology each time, Emily wondered if the contact was always entirely accidental.

She knew that her reactions to his touches were hardly ordinary. Each time, her pulse tripped, her throat tightened, her breath hitched slightly in her throat. She only hoped that none of the too-perceptive observers around her—most particularly, Wade him-self—noticed her embarrassingly juvenile behavior.

She was all but hyperventilating over the man, for goodness' sake. In front of her relatives and her minis-ter!

"What's this I hear about you selling your house, Emily?" Jennie Tatum asked curiously, looking as if she'd been waiting for the right opportunity to broach the subject.

This was probably the juiciest piece of gossip that had hit Honoria in weeks, outside of the food fight at the fall festival. Emily imagined that everyone would be speculating about her plans.

"Yes," she said, wondering how many times in the next few months she would conduct this same conver-sation. "A four-bedroom house on twenty acres is more than I want to keep up for myself."

Marvella clucked her tongue. "That property has been in your family for generations, Emily. Are you sure you want to let it go?"

"I've given this a lot of thought, Marvella. This is what I want to do." Emily spoke with a firmness that was as much meant to convince Wade as the others, since she didn't want him to reconsider his interest in the house.

But Marvella didn't look reassured. "Family history is so important, dear. Are you sure you want to just give yours away? What about your own children? Haven't you considered hanging onto the place for their sakes?"

"I don't have any children, Marvella," Emily re-minded her gently. "And I'm not giving my home away. I'm selling it."

"Yes, and I'm going to make sure she gets a fair price for it," Caleb inserted.

Wade chuckled. "No doubt," he murmured.

"Where are you going to live when you sell your house, Emily?" Brother Tatum asked. "Do you have a place in mind?"

"I'm considering my options," Emily replied vaguely. She knew very well what would happen if she admitted that she had no plans beyond getting away from Honoria. They would be horrified. Poor, parentless Emily, on her own in the big, bad world with no one to guide her.

"I told Miss Emily she can live with me and my daddy," Clay said, speaking up for the first time since the conversation had begun. "We'd like that, wouldn't we, Daddy?"

A sudden silence fell around the table. Emily felt her last bite of cola-basted ham lodge in her throat.

The only one who seemed oblivious to the awkward pause was Marvella, who drained half her glass of iced tea, set it down with a thump, and said, "I hope you aren't selling because you've started worrying about the crime in Honoria."

Emily lifted an eyebrow. "Hardly," she said a bit dryly. "We barely have any crime in Honoria, Marvella."

"What about all those houses that were robbed during the fall festival? And I hear there was another robbery two nights ago, while the family was at the junior-high football game. You doing anything about those, Chief Davenport?"

"Everything we can, ma'am," he answered patiently. "I have my two best officers investigating, and

I've stepped up patrols as much as I can, considering our limited staff.''

"Ask me, you should check out that youngest O'Brien boy. He's as wild as they come. I just know he's the one that's been stealing traffic signs around here, and spray-painting all the nice buildings.''

"We're checking out all leads, Ms. Tucker. Whoever is doing this will get caught, I promise you.''

Marvella nodded. "Good. And when you catch 'em, you make sure they get more than a slap on the wrist, you hear? Let 'em know we don't put up with that nonsense in our town.''

"Yes, ma'am,'' Wade agreed, his meek tone making Emily smile.

"Tell me about your family, Mrs. McBride,'' Wade said, quickly changing the subject. "You have three grown children?''

Bobbie answered without hesitation. "Yes, a daughter and two sons. Tara, the eldest, is a tax attorney in Atlanta.''

"Followed in her father's footsteps, did she?'' Wade asked with a smile directed toward Caleb.

Caleb answered. "Oh, she's no country lawyer like her old man. Tara graduated with honors from Harvard. She worked for a big firm in Atlanta for several years. Now she and a partner have gone into business on their own.''

"She's getting married next month,'' Bobbie added, shaking her head with apparent bemusement. "To a private investigator named Blake Fox. He's a charming man, though a bit...different.''

"I like him,'' Emily said, smiling as she remembered

her recent meeting with her cousin's gorgeous and somewhat offbeat fiancé.

"And your sons?" Wade asked, seeming to make sure the conversation stayed away from Emily's personal plans—or his own—for a while.

Emily sent Wade a grateful look as Bobbie launched into a proud monologue about her sons and her brilliant and adorable grandson, Sam.

BOBBIE SERVED apricot-nectar cake with ice cream for dessert, and then, finally the meal was over. Typically, the women moved to the kitchen to clean up while Caleb led the guys into the den for football and coffee.

"I think he likes you, Emily," Bobbie whispered loudly as they loaded dirty dishes into the dishwasher.

Her cheeks warming, Emily gave her aunt a warning glance. "Aunt Bobbie..."

"He did seem rather taken, didn't he?" Marvella said approvingly.

"I thought I noticed some interest there." The minister's wife seemed as prone to matchmaking as her friends. "You and Chief Davenport would make a nice couple, Emily. He's widowed, you know. And that boy of his already seems very fond of you."

"But—"

"Clay's a precious little boy, isn't he?" Bobbie mused. "So polite. The chief is doing a fine job of raising him."

"I hear that housekeeper of his is a wonder," Marvella, who missed little local gossip despite her advanced years, commented. "LouAnne Garner took a casserole over to welcome them to town, and she said you could eat off'n the floors, the house was so clean.

She takes good care of little Clay when his daddy's at work, too. She's Mexican, you know."

"She's rather shy, I think," Jennie confided. "I invited her to church, but she said she's Catholic, so I told her about St. Joseph's."

"Have you met her yet, Emily?" Bobbie wanted to know.

"Of course not, Aunt Bobbie. I hardly know Chief Davenport. I've had no reason to meet his housekeeper."

The women brushed off Emily's protestations without visible concern.

"I wouldn't be surprised if the chief invites you out for dinner or a movie real soon," Marvella advised Emily. "You let him know right off that you're a nice girl, you hear?"

Emily's cheeks flushed hotter. "Er—"

"Now, Marvella, I'm sure he knows that already," Jennie murmured.

Marvella stuck to her opinion. "A lady has to make things clear these days. And I'm sure Emily doesn't mind a little advice, since she doesn't have a mother around to guide her. Isn't that right, dear?"

Bobbie lifted her chin. "I've always been available for Emily, just as I was for my own daughter. Emily and I have had some long talks about young men, haven't we, sweetheart?"

To Emily's mingled embarrassment and gratitude, they certainly had. Bobbie had always tried to fill the gaping void left in Emily's young life when her mother had run off with Al Jennings. Still, while Emily loved her aunt for her solicitude, she certainly didn't want to discuss such things now.

"Let me clean this pan for you, Aunt Bobbie," she said, making a rather desperate grab for the dishwashing liquid. "I'll just wash it in the sink."

"Watch your jewelry," Jennie Tatum warned. "You'll mess up your watch, if you aren't careful. And that lovely bracelet."

Emily glanced automatically at the heavy gold bracelet on her right wrist. "I'll be careful."

Looking at the bracelet with a slight frown between her pencilled brows, Emily's aunt asked, "Where did you get that, Emily? I don't remember seeing you wear it before—but, for some reason, it looks familiar to me."

"I've worn it a couple of times before," Emily said, uncomfortable again with the turn the conversation had taken. "It was my mother's, I think. I—er—found it after Dad died."

She had no intention of telling them about finding the bracelet hidden in the "time capsule." She'd spent weeks fretting over it after her father's funeral. Wondering how the bracelet had gotten into the box. And who else had known about their time capsule.

She had finally decided that she must have put it there herself, and had then forgotten. She'd been so young. She'd probably found the bracelet somewhere among her father's things, thought it was pretty, and had tucked it into her treasure cache and forgotten about it. How else could it possibly have gotten into a buried box she'd packed herself?

Though she'd never consciously intended to wear the bracelet since she'd discovered it in the box, she'd found herself slipping it on one morning as she'd gotten ready for work. It had felt...right, somehow, on her wrist. She'd worn it several times since, deliberately giving little thought to the significance of wearing something that had belonged to the mother who'd abandoned her when she was still in diapers.

Suddenly, Bobbie's eyes widened. "Oh, goodness, I *do* remember that bracelet. Nadine loved it so much I never saw her without it. She would never say who gave it to her, though I knew it wasn't Josiah. I always assumed it was...er..."

"Al Jennings," Emily said quietly, naming the married man with whom her mother had disappeared so many years ago.

Bobbie nodded. "I would have thought she'd have taken it with her. As I said, I never saw her without it."

"She must have left it for Emily," Marvella said, studying the bracelet intently.

"She probably did," Bobbie agreed, apparently struck by the suggestion. "You know, I never could understand how Nadine could leave her baby girl that way. I didn't blame her so much for leaving Josiah—everyone knew they were all wrong for each other—but to run off with another woman's husband, leaving all those children behind...well, I could hardly believe it."

"A gold bracelet is hardly compensation for the loss of a mother, is it, Emily?" Jennie Tatum asked sympathetically.

"No." The bracelet felt suddenly heavy on Emily's arm. "It isn't."

"Excuse me, ladies."

Wade's voice from the doorway made the group of women fall silent. Emily turned to look at him, wondering just how much he'd overheard. He wasn't looking at her, but at her aunt.

"Mrs. McBride, I wanted to thank you for having Clay and me to lunch. We enjoyed it very much."

"Oh, are you leaving, Chief?"

"Yes, ma'am. We have a few other things to do this afternoon. And I'm going to be checking into the progress of the investigation of those break-ins, Mrs. Tucker."

Marvella nodded in satisfaction. "Good. You find those miscreants, you hear?"

"Yes, ma'am. Good afternoon, Mrs. Tatum."

"Good afternoon, Chief."

Only then did Wade glance at Emily. "See you, Emily."

"See you, Wade."

Both the words and their attitudes were quite casual, implying nothing beyond friendly acquaintance. Emily couldn't imagine why the older women were suddenly smiling at her with such indulgent approval.

7

IT WAS A BEAUTIFUL Sunday evening. Crisp. Clear. Fragrant.

Emily sat on her porch swing after dark, sipping a steaming mug of instant cappuccino and enjoying the weather. She wasn't expecting company, so she was surprised when a vehicle suddenly turned into her driveway.

Her pulse accelerated when she recognized Wade Davenport's Jeep. What was he doing here? She'd only seen him a few hours ago.

She waited on the swing while he climbed out of his Jeep and ambled toward her with his usual, unhurried stride. "Evening, Miz Emily," he drawled, tugging at his forelock.

She couldn't help smiling at his clowning. "Evening, Chief Davenport," she replied in the same lazy, Southern drawl that came so naturally to them. "I didn't expect to see you again so soon."

"I wanted to talk to you, if you've got a minute."

"I've got several minutes. Can I get you anything? Coffee? Iced tea?"

"No, thanks. I just had dinner."

Emily set her empty coffee mug on the porch and scooted all the way to one side of the small swing, allowing room for Wade to sit beside her. He practically filled up the remaining space, leaving only an inch or so between them. Close enough to make her skin tingle.

She spoke quickly, needing to fill the silence between them. "What did you want to talk to me about, Wade?"

He pulled one knee slightly upward, and wrapped his hands around it, using his other foot to set the swing into gentle motion. "I'm planning to make an offer for your house tomorrow."

Did he want to discuss the price? She moistened her lips, wondering what to say. She'd never handled a sale like this before, and wasn't certain of the protocol. She remembered her uncle's warning for her to get a fair market price—but she'd trusted Mary Kay to help her determine that. "What about it?"

"Emily, are you *really* sure you want to sell?"

She sighed. "You've been thinking about what Marvella said at lunch, haven't you?"

"I couldn't help thinking about it. She's the one who pointed out that the place has been in your family for a very long time. You've got a nice house here and a lot of good land. What if you decide in a few months that you've made a terrible mistake?"

"Wade, I've been thinking about this for years. I've talked to you about this already. The whole time Dad was ill, when I had no choice but to remain here, I told myself that as soon as I was free, I wanted to get away. This house, this town, are all I've known all my life. I feel almost as though I've been caged here while all my cousins and most of my childhood friends were free to fly off to exciting new places."

"I've been to a lot of other places. They aren't as exciting as you might think."

"I'd like to find that out for myself," she insisted.

"Where will you go when you move out? What will you do?"

She shrugged. "I don't know. I'll have the money from the sale to live on for a while. The house is paid for, so I don't owe anything. Combined with Dad's insurance, I'll have enough to tide me over until I decide where I want to settle down and what I want to do."

"Where will you go first?"

"I was thinking about New York. I've never been to New York, though I've always wanted to visit there. I want to see some Broadway shows, and go through the Metropolitan Museum and eat at the Tavern on the Green. Maybe even go to the top of the Empire State Building. All the things I've heard about in movies and on television."

"Alone?"

She nodded. "Sure. Why not?"

"You want a list of reasons? I've been to New York, Emily. And, while it's an exciting and fascinating city, it can be a dangerous place for a young woman alone. Especially a woman who has little experience with big cities."

She refused to be discouraged by his warning. "I'll be fine. There are plenty of single women my age who live and work in the city. We only hear so much about the bad things on the news because it makes good copy."

"That may be true, but remember that I'm a cop. I spent some time training in one of the precincts in New York. I know the kind of crime that goes on there. It's a hell of a lot worse than the few break-ins and petty vandalism we've had around here."

"I'm not entirely naive. I know what to expect."

"I'm not so sure that you do," he argued grimly.

She swallowed another sigh. "Wade, I have a big brother—somewhere. I really don't need another one."

Wade went suddenly still, stopping the swing's lulling motion. "Have I given you the impression that my feelings toward you are fraternal? If so, you've gotten the wrong idea. Completely wrong."

Emily felt her heart skip a beat in response to something she heard in his deep voice. "Um—"

"Trust me, Emily McBride, I don't think of you as a little sister. And I sure don't want you looking at me as a big brother."

She cleared her throat. "I, er—"

He twisted on the swing until he was facing her. And then he reached out and took her hand, which had gone icy. His felt almost blazing hot in contrast.

"My reasons for wanting you to stay in Honoria aren't entirely professional. Nor are they unselfish. Sure, I'm concerned for your safety. But there's a hell of a lot more to it than that."

She tried to think of something intelligent to say. Heck, she'd have settled for coherent.

Wade didn't give her a chance. He leaned closer, his breath warm on her face when he murmured, "I've been wanting to do this since the first minute I saw you. If you want me to back off, now's your chance to say so."

Maybe she would have—if she had been capable of speaking at all. As it was, she could only close her eyes and try not to be completely swept away when his lips covered hers.

She wasn't entirely successful.

Play the
"LAS VEGAS"
Game
and get
3 FREE GIFTS!

1. Pull back all 3 tabs on the card at right. Then check the claim chart to see what we have for you — 2 FREE BOOKS and a gift — ALL YOURS! ALL FREE!

2. Send back this card and you'll receive brand-new Harlequin Temptation® novels. These books have a cover price of $3.75 each, but they are yours to keep absolutely free.

3. There's no catch. You're under no obligation to buy anything. We charge nothing — ZERO — for your first shipment. And you don't have to make any minimum number of purchases — not even one!

4. The fact is thousands of readers enjoy receiving books by mail from the Harlequin Reader Service™. They like the convenience of home delivery... they like getting the best new novels BEFORE they're available in stores... and they love our discount prices!

5. We hope that after receiving your free books you'll want to remain a subscriber. But the choice is yours — to continue or cancel, any time at all! So why not take us up on our invitation, with no risk of any kind. You'll be glad you did!

Yours Free!

FREE!
No Obligation to Buy!
No Purchase Necessary!

Play the

"**LAS VEGAS**" Game

> **PEEL BACK HERE ▶**
> **PEEL BACK HERE ▶**
> **PEEL BACK HERE ▶**

YES! I have pulled back the 3 tabs. Please send me all the free
Harlequin Temptation® books and the gift for which I qualify.
I understand that I am under no obligation to purchase any
books, as explained on the back and opposite page.

(U-H-T-05/98)   **142 HDL CF7Z**

NAME   (PLEASE PRINT CLEARLY)

ADDRESS   APT.

CITY   STATE   ZIP

7	7	7	**GET 2 FREE BOOKS & A FREE MYSTERY GIFT!**	Offer limited to one per household and not valid to current Harlequin Temptation® subscribers. All orders subject to approval.
🍀	🍀	🍀	**GET 2 FREE BOOKS!**	
🍒	🍒	🍒	**GET 1 FREE BOOK!**	
🔔	🔔	🔔	**TRY AGAIN!**	PRINTED IN U.S.A.

BUSINESS REPLY MAIL

FIRST-CLASS MAIL   PERMIT NO. 717   BUFFALO NY

POSTAGE WILL BE PAID BY ADDRESSEE

HARLEQUIN READER SERVICE
3010 WALDEN AVE
PO BOX 1867
BUFFALO NY 14240-9952

NO POSTAGE
NECESSARY
IF MAILED
IN THE
UNITED STATES

Wade's lips were firm and warm against hers, bold and skilled. And Emily could no more resist responding to him than she could stop her heart from pounding in her chest.

Wade took his time kissing her. Tasting her. Exploring every centimeter of her mouth. When he finally drew back, it was with a reluctance he didn't bother to hide.

Dazed, Emily looked up at him, realizing for the first time that she'd clutched his denim jacket in both hands and was holding on to him for dear life. "Okay," she said, her voice shaky. "I'll knock five thousand off the house."

His laugh was rough edged. "No, you won't, and you know that isn't why I kissed you."

Yes, she knew, but she'd thought it safer to try to make a joke—no matter how weak—than to let him realize exactly how seriously she'd taken that kiss.

"Do you believe me now that I don't see you as a little sister?"

She released her grip on his jacket and locked her hands together tightly in her lap. "Yes. But—"

"Then I've accomplished something tonight, anyway."

"Wade, I'm very serious about leaving town. I've been planning this for years."

He nodded. "So you've said."

"And I still think it would be a mistake for us to get...involved. Considering that I'm leaving, and everything," she said lamely.

"Yes, we've agreed on that, as well."

"It's really for the best. It's not as if we...well, you know...clicked or anything." Oh, she was sounding lamer by the minute, she thought with a swallowed groan.

He tugged her into his arms and covered her mouth with his again before she had a chance to react. Not that she would have stopped him if she could have, she thought, drifting into another spectacular kiss.

An eternity later, he drew slowly back, his smile wicked. "I think I heard some definite clicking."

Her cheeks flamed. "You know what I mean," she muttered.

"Honey, I'm not even sure *you* know what you mean."

She bit her lip. He was probably right. And it didn't help that her pulse had tripped again just because he'd called her "honey."

This was no way to keep her emotional distance from him.

She took the coward's way out. "It's getting late. You'd better go."

"So I should make the offer on your house?"

"If you don't, someone else will," she said, trying to sound matter-of-fact about it. "The place is still for sale."

He nodded and stood, making the swing sway. Emily planted her feet on the porch to steady it.

"Good night, Emily."

"Good night, Wade."

"I'll be seeing you around."

She didn't know whether to take his words as a promise—or a warning.

LONG AFTER WADE had driven away, Emily stood in her living room, holding the colorful brochures she'd collected during the past few years. Exotic names swam before her eyes. Antigua. New Zealand. Brussels. Venice. Wales.

She had never intended to try to visit them all, but just looking at the pictures and reading the descriptions had given her pleasure. During those years when her only travel had consisted of driving from home to work and back again, she'd escaped into daydreams of wandering around the world, experiencing places and people and foods and customs that she'd only read about in books and magazines.

Now that she had the freedom and finances to actually make some of those daydreams come true, she would be a fool to throw away all her plans just because a good-looking, smooth-talking police chief—who packed pure dynamite in his kisses, by the way—had come to town.

EMILY WAS SUMMONED to her boss's office again late on Monday afternoon.

Half expecting to see Sam Jennings and the intriguing chief of police again, she walked warily into Marshall Hayes's office.

To Emily's relief, Hayes was the only one in the room.

He smiled when she entered. "Hello, Emily."

She made a show of looking in the corners of the wood-paneled office. "No gendarmes waiting to haul me off to the big house?"

Hayes chuckled in response to her lame attempt at humor. "Actually, it's the opposite. Chief Davenport just called. He had some news for us concerning his investigation."

Emily's heart gave a little flutter—only because she was a bit nervous about the contents of that call, she assured herself. "Was the call about Mr. Jennings's accusation?"

"Yes. Apparently, Sam Jennings has finally found evidence that Tammy Powell had been bilking him for some time. Several thousand dollars were involved. It's obvious that she falsified the deposit records to hide her tracks."

"Does this mean I've been completely cleared?" Emily was almost afraid to hope.

Marshall Hayes nodded firmly. "Completely. Not that I ever had any doubt," he added.

Emily smiled at the kindly man who'd been her employer for so long. "Thank you. Your trust means a great deal to me."

Embarrassed by the show of emotion, Hayes shrugged. "I thought you would be anxious to know that everything's been settled and that you have nothing more to worry about."

"Thank you. It's a great relief to know that I'm no longer under suspicion."

He nodded again and returned to his seat behind his desk. "You've handled this whole thing very well. The first of next month, I'm giving you a raise. It's time for you to have one, anyway. You're a valuable asset to our team."

Feeling just a bit guilty, Emily held onto her smile. She hadn't yet told her employer of her plans to leave Honoria. She had wanted to get the sale of her house fully underway before giving notice at the bank. "That's very kind of you."

He gave her a wry smile. "You should get an apology from Sam Jennings, but I wouldn't advise you to hold your breath."

"No. I don't think that would be advisable," she replied, her tone equally dry.

Hayes pulled a stack of paperwork in front of him. "I won't keep you any longer. I'm sure you have things to do."

As Emily went back to work, it occurred to her that, since the investigation was over, there was no official reason for her to see Wade Davenport again. And she told herself that it was utterly ridiculous to feel even a twinge of disappointment that the embezzlement case was now closed. She should be thrilled that she was no longer a suspect. That she was free, once and for all, to leave this town and its convoluted history behind her.

So why was she suddenly feeling a bit depressed?

THE NEXT TIME Wade saw Emily, she had blood dripping from two deep, ugly puncture marks in her neck. Her skin was a ghastly white, with dark purple hollows beneath her eyes. Blood had pooled around the corners of her mouth, and her hair was a tangled mess around her death-mask face.

She had obviously been the victim of a most heinous crime.

"Damn," Wade said. "I was kinda hopin' to be the one to take a bite out of your neck."

He saw a bright pink flush spread beneath her stark white makeup, spoiling the dramatic effect. Her eyes darted from side to side, obviously checking to make sure there had been no eavesdroppers.

It was a week before Halloween, and full dress rehearsal was underway for the Community League's haunted house. Wade had stopped by on his way home from the office primarily because he'd known she would be there.

He'd missed seeing her. He hadn't been able to stop thinking about her during the two weeks that had passed since he had kissed her. He had deliberately stayed away from her after his quick call to her employer to let her know that she had been officially cleared in the Jennings case.

Emily had made it obvious that she had no intention of allowing Wade to change her mind about leaving, and he'd told himself that he had no time to begin something he couldn't finish. Yet, no matter how many times he tried to convince himself that he should forget about her and get on with his life, he still found himself lying in bed in the middle of the night, reliving those kisses. Wanting to kiss her again.

Wanting more.

"Wade," she said, both her voice and her smile a bit strained. "What are you doing here?"

"Just thought I'd see how things were coming along." He glanced around the ticket lobby, which was bustling with ghoulish characters and people in work clothes carrying hammers and paintbrushes for last-minute touch-ups to the scenery. Someone was shouting directions, but no one seemed to be listening. "A bit hectic, isn't it?"

"Things always are, at this stage." She ran her hands down the sides of her floating white dress, which was dotted with make-believe blood from her fake injuries. Wade found it very interesting that she was still so skittish around him. Maybe she couldn't forget their kisses, either.

"Grand opening is tomorrow night?"

She nodded. "Yes. At seven."

"I'll have to bring Clay."

She looked doubtful.

Wade lifted an eyebrow. "You don't think that's a good idea?"

"It's going to be pretty scary. Do you think Clay's old enough to handle it?"

"Well..." Wade looked around at the townspeople dressed up so gruesomely. "I thought he would understand that the characters are just people in costume."

"They look that way now, but when the lighting is turned down and the scary music and sound effects begin, and everyone is screaming and wailing for atmosphere, it can get pretty intense. I've seen adults come out of these things shaken. And when my cousin took her twins through a haunted house when they were about Clay's age, she said she had to deal with nightmares for weeks. Of course, you know your son better than I do."

"And you know this haunted house better than I do," he returned. "I didn't realize it was going to be so scary."

"It's designed primarily for teenagers. Some smaller kids will go through, but I think you should be prepared for what to expect if you decide to bring Clay."

"Thanks. I'll keep that in mind."

"Okay, everyone, places!" the woman directing the cast shouted through cupped hands. "We're going to have a dry run. Chief Davenport, would you like to be our first victim...er, guest?"

Wade grinned. "Sure. That sounds like fun."

Emily murmured something he didn't quite catch and ran off to take her place with the others.

It turned out that Wade was one of five test guests, as the director, whose name Wade thought was Tressie something-or-other, referred to them. The other four were teenagers, who were introduced to Wade as Jessica, Shelly, Scott and Adam. The girls giggled and the boys postured while Tressie, who would be serving as their guide through the haunted house, gave them what she explained would be the standard entrance spiel.

"Please don't touch any of the characters," she said. "They will get close to you, but they won't touch you. We have to say that," she murmured to Wade, "because sometimes the macho guys going through actually punch the performers. Can you believe it?"

"If that should happen, give my office a call," he replied firmly, hating the thought of Emily being hurt just because she'd tried to raise money for charity.

Tressie nodded and returned to her monologue. "No smoking is allowed inside the building. Please stay with the group. It will be dark inside and you could be injured if you wander off the designated pathway. If you need assistance during the tour, feel free to speak to Mary, your back guide," she pointed to a shy-looking young woman who blushed when everyone looked at her. "Mostly, we want you to have a good time...and be scared out of your socks," she added with a grin. "Any questions before we begin? No? Okay, then it's time to enter the Trail of Terror."

From hidden speakers, eerie music suddenly began to play, underscored by creepy sound effects such as creaking doors, howling dogs, crazed laughter, and shivery screams. Wade noted that one of the girls—Jessica, he thought—looked suddenly nervous. He smiled reassuringly when she took a step closer to him.

"I've never been to one of these things," she confided in a whisper.

"It should be fun," he replied. "You probably know nearly everyone inside."

"Yes," she agreed doubtfully. "But they look different in that weird makeup."

"You'll be fine," Wade promised.

"You ain't scared, are you, Jessica?" Scott taunted, holding his shoulders back to prove that haunted houses were nothing to him. "This is sissy stuff. Grown-ups in Halloween costumes."

"I'm not scared," Jessica insisted, lifting her chin. "I've just never been to one before."

"Ladies and gentlemen." Tressie swept an arm dramatically toward the entrance. "Shall we begin?"

The group passed through a doorway covered in strips of hanging black gauze, leaving the dimly lighted lobby area behind to step into total darkness. They immediately bumped into each other, causing the teens to gasp and giggle. The guide instructed them to place their right hands on the wall to keep them on track as they moved slowly forward.

One of the girls squealed after taking only a few steps. "E-e-w-w," she said. "There's something gross on the wall."

A moment later Wade's fingers brushed something furry and rather sticky that had apparently been glued to the wall. He grinned. That was clever.

They passed several gory, strangely illuminated scenes. The undead rose from open coffins, werewolves howled at the tour group, mad scientists conducted gruesome experiments on bloody body parts—which, on closer inspection, appeared to be professional stage props—and Dr. Frankenstein tried to animate his creature with jolts of flickering blue light. The girls screamed when half human, half animal creatures resembling those on Dr. Moreau's island dashed toward them, stopped only inches away by the chains on their legs.

The boys teased the girls mercilessly about being scared, only to jump half a foot each when several particularly nasty looking creatures rose unexpectedly from piles of hay to make menacing looking grabs for the boys. Jessica and Shelly hooted. Wade couldn't help chuckling.

Looked like the Community League had a winner on their hands, he thought.

And then he saw Emily.

An oily-haired vampire leaned over her, his gleaming fangs poised to sink yet again into her already bleeding neck. Emily was draped back over his arm, her tangled curls tumbling behind her, her slender body outlined by the clinging white dress she wore. She played her part to the hilt. She looked genuinely terrified, her blue eyes wide with feigned anguish.

Wade found it ruefully amusing that his first instinct was to rush to her rescue. He had to push his hands into his pockets to keep them from reaching out toward the guy who held her.

Suddenly he felt as foolish as the giggling teenagers surrounding him.

The vampire looked up at them, eyes glowing red in the eerie light, fangs gleaming. "Get out," he hissed, obviously enraged by the interruption of his feast. "Go away!"

The teenagers complied hastily, hurrying toward the next exhibit. Wade lingered just long enough to look at Emily with a raised eyebrow, causing her to ruin the effect of her scene by breaking into a sudden smile. Pleased with himself, he moved on.

"THE POLICE CHIEF'S got his eye on you, Emily," Bob, the evil vampire, teased as soon as the tour group was out of hearing. "I think he wants you."

Blushing, Emily disentangled herself from Bob's arms. "Don't be ridiculous," she chided the computer programmer she'd known since they'd both been in Mrs. Burton's kindergarten class. "Chief Davenport and I hardly know each other."

"He knows you well enough to have a thing for you," Bob retorted. "I thought he was going to go for *my* throat when he saw me pretending to attack you."

Emily reminded herself that Bob had always been an inveterate tease, that he enjoyed watching people squirm. She really shouldn't give him that satisfaction, she thought, but...

"Weren't we supposed to meet everyone else in the lobby when our scene was completed?" she asked, firmly changing the subject.

"Yeah. We're all going out for pizza. Hey, you want me to ask the chief if he wants to join us? I'll be real subtle about it. He'll never know it's a fix-up for you and him."

Bob was about as subtle as a sledgehammer. Even if she wanted to be "fixed up" with Wade—which she assuredly did not—she wouldn't want Bob having anything to do with it.

She spoke coolly, determined to squelch this before it went any further. "I'm sure Wade is anxious to get home to his son. And I have things I have to do at home this evening. I won't be able to join you for the pizza party."

"No, really, Emily. He seems like a nice guy. He's available. There aren't a whole lot of single men our age in Honoria, especially now that Carl Evans and I have both gotten paired off. You ought to think about it."

"Bob, I'm perfectly capable of taking care of my own social life," she replied stiffly. "Please don't say anything more about it. Now, if you'll excuse me, I'm going to join the others in the lobby."

She stalked away from him without another word, easily negotiating the dark corridors that led back to the lobby. She'd been through them enough to know her way by now.

She wondered why on earth everyone in town suddenly seemed to have decided that she and Wade belonged together.

They couldn't be more wrong, of course.

8

NOVEMBER SWEPT into Honoria with a line of thunderstorms that rattled windows, battered the remaining leaves off the trees, and drove the townspeople indoors for hot drinks and long evenings of television and conversation. The haunted house had been a great success, but a thoroughly exhausting one. Emily was relieved that it was over, though she'd had a great time scaring most of the teenagers and many of the adults of the surrounding communities.

Wade's offer on Emily's house had been made and accepted. Once his loan had been approved and all the formalities of transferring property from one owner to another had been completed, the house and land would belong to him. Emily thought it should all be finalized by the end of the month. He'd leased his current house through the end of the year, so she had until then to move out.

It gave her a funny feeling to realize that by January, she would basically be homeless.

She reminded herself yet again that this had been her choice.

By the third wet, stormy day in a row—a Thursday—tempers in town began to fray. Emily noticed it at the bank, where her customers with their frizzy, damp hair and water-spotted clothes demonstrated considerably less patience than usual. She had to make a special effort to maintain her own, and she felt that her smile grew increasingly strained as the day went on. She was relieved when the workday ended and she was free to go home.

She had driven all of three blocks when she remembered that she had used the last scrap of her last bar of soap that morning in the shower. She groaned, and wondered half-seriously for a moment if she could just use dishwashing detergent in the morning. Which only reminded her that she was out of that, too.

She sighed. "Looks like I'm going to have to get wet," she muttered, and pulled into the crowded parking lot of the town's sole discount store. After circling futilely in search of a parking space close to the door, she parked some distance away, pulling an umbrella from the back seat. The rain was coming down in torrents, and she didn't expect the umbrella to accomplish much, but it was better than nothing.

She dashed through the downpour, protecting her head as much as possible, ruefully aware that the hems of her dark slacks were getting soaked. Cold water seeped through the thin leather of her shoes, chilling her from the toes up. *What a rotten afternoon*, she thought morosely.

She made her selections quickly, gathering only what she needed for the next day, since she didn't want to carry too much through the rain. And then she rounded the end of an aisle and nearly ran smack into Sam Jennings, whom she hadn't seen since he'd made his accusations several weeks earlier.

Jennings stepped back quickly to keep her from barreling into him. "Hey, watch where you're going."

Emily had thrown out a hand to steady herself against him, clutching automatically at his arm. Her heavy gold bracelet clinked as she quickly drew away, not wanting to touch him any more than necessary. The sound drew his attention and his scowl deepened. Emily couldn't imagine why the sight of her bracelet always seemed to enrage him.

"I'm sorry, Dr. Jennings," she said, making an effort to be cordial. "I didn't see you."

"Hmmph."

She supposed that was as close as he would come to accepting her apology.

"Excuse me." She stepped sideways to move around him.

"I hear you and the police chief are seeing a lot of each other these days. Guess I know now why he was so anxious to clear you of any involvement in the theft of my money."

Jennings's sarcastic words stopped Emily in her tracks. "I beg your pardon?" she asked, turning again to face him.

He shrugged. "You didn't do it, I believe that now. All I'm saying is that if you had, I'm not so sure the chief would have done anything about it. But then, you McBrides are used to that sort of special treatment by the local authorities, aren't you? After all, your brother got away with murder."

"Why, you—"

Emily had to force herself not to give in to sheer instinct and slap the arrogant look right off Sam Jennings's florid face. But she had no intention of letting his ugly words go unchallenged.

She took a step toward him, letting the full extent of

her anger show in her expression. She had the satisfaction of seeing some of the cocky arrogance leave his face as he took an involuntary step backward.

"I have had enough of your insinuations, Sam Jennings," she warned him, her voice shaking with rage. "If I hear one more accusation from you, I'll slap you with a lawsuit so fast your head will spin. And never mention my brother in my presence again, is that clear? You aren't good enough to speak Lucas's name."

She stepped backward, as far away from him as possible. And then she turned without another word and stalked away.

One day, she thought furiously, Sam Jennings would get what he deserved. She only wished she would be around to see it, but most likely she would be gone by then.

In a couple of months, she promised herself, she would never have to see Sam Jennings again—or anyone else who disliked her family.

Maybe she'd been wavering lately, wondering if she was really doing the right thing...and maybe Wade Davenport played a part in her indecision. But this incident with Jennings reinforced her belief that getting out of Honoria was the only way she was ever going to find the happiness that had eluded her during the past fifteen years.

EMILY HAD HARDLY arrived home on Friday evening when the telephone began to ring. Somehow knowing it would be someone wanting a favor, she sighed heavily before picking it up. She'd been so glad to see the weekend begin, thinking she had two whole days all to herself. "Hello?"

"Emily, it's Wade. I need a favor."

She'd been prepared for the reason behind the call, but not for the identity of the caller.

"Wade. What can I do for you?" she asked, assuming his call was about the sale of the house.

"I really hate to ask this. If I had any other choice..."

"Wade, please. Just ask."

He sighed through the phone lines. "Would it be possible for Clay to spend the night with you tonight? I wouldn't ask, of course, but Cecilia left this morning for a weekend with her family, and I've been called to Atlanta on an emergency. I have to leave as soon as I can make arrangements for Clay."

"Of course he can stay with me. I hope the emergency isn't anyone in your family?"

"No, it's a case I worked on with Atlanta CID. Everything's unraveling on it, and I've been called on for assistance. It's critical that I get there as soon as I can, or I would have waited until tomorrow."

"Of course. Bring him on over. We'll have a great time together. And don't bother to feed him. I'll make dinner."

"I don't know how to tell you how much I appreciate this. I feel really rotten for dumping this on you, but you were the only one I knew Clay would feel comfortable staying with overnight...at least until we get to know everyone around here a little better. He has a couple of friends from school, but I didn't feel that I knew their parents well enough yet to ask them."

Emily thought it a bit unnerving that he'd felt he knew her well enough to entrust her with the care of his son. Every time she tried to convince herself that there was no special connection between her and Wade, he did something that suggested otherwise.

"Bring him over, Wade," she repeated, not knowing what else to say. "You still have a long drive ahead of you."

WADE PULLED into her driveway less than half an hour later. Emily had the door open before he could ring the bell. She noted that Wade was holding a child's suitcase in one hand and Clay's hand in his other.

Clay looked rather uncertain. Emily could certainly understand that; the child hardly knew her. And now his father was dropping him off to spend the entire night with her.

She immediately smiled to put him at ease. "Hi, Clay. I understand you and I are going to have a slumber party this evening."

Holding a rather ragged stuffed tiger in the crook of his right arm, Clay nodded. "Daddy has to go to Atlanta for a meeting."

"Yes, he told me. I hope you don't mind staying with me. I'm certainly looking forward to having you as my guest."

"It's just for tonight," he reminded her. "Daddy's coming back tomorrow."

"Then we'll make the most of it, okay? I have some videos and some games, and I thought I'd make homemade pizza for dinner. Do you like pizza?"

"With pepperoni?" Clay asked hopefully, taking a small step toward her.

"Definitely with pepperoni. And did I mention that I own all three _Star Wars_ films on video?"

"Okay, Daddy, you can go now," Clay announced,

releasing his father's hand to reach for Emily's. "We'll be fine."

Wade chuckled and looked ironically at Emily. "Looks like you've cast your spell on yet another Davenport male," he murmured. "Just how do you do that?"

She gave him a quelling look. "Shouldn't you be on your way, Wade? You said they're waiting for you in Atlanta?"

He held up his right hand in a gesture of surrender. "Okay. I can take a hint. Thanks again, Emily. I owe you big-time."

Emily suddenly, and unwillingly, thought of Sam Jennings. What would he say if he heard the chief of police assert that he "owed" her—"big-time"?

Which only proved that she'd allowed Jennings's rude and unprovoked attack on her yesterday to bother her much more than it should have.

EMILY AND CLAY made and ate pizza together, then followed that by nestling onto the couch with popcorn to watch a *Star Wars* video—the first one, which they agreed was the best of the three. Emily was amused to learn that Clay could quote whole passages of dialogue.

"How many times have you seen these films?" she asked.

He shrugged. "Millions."

"And what is it that you like so much about them?"

He looked blank for a moment, then said, "'Cause they're exciting."

She supposed that was reason enough for an eight-year-old boy.

"Yes, they are," she assured him gravely.

Clay rubbed his eyes. "It's getting kind of late, isn't it?"

"Mmm-hmm." Emily made a show of smothering a yawn behind her hand. "Goodness, I'm getting sleepy. Are you?"

"Just a little. Where am I going to sleep?"

"In the bedroom next to mine. The one you liked when you toured the house with your daddy—the one with the window seat?"

Clay's face brightened. "I remember. I told Daddy I want that to be my room if we move here."

Again, Emily was aware of that funny little pang at the thought of someone else living in her house. It wasn't that she couldn't envision Wade and Clay living here—she simply couldn't imagine herself *not* living here.

That was something she was going to have to work on.

Emily sent Clay to brush his teeth and change into pajamas. And then she boosted him into the big bed in the room he'd claimed for his own. He held his stuffed tiger tightly in one arm. Emily tucked the covers carefully around both boy and tiger.

"I'll leave the night-light on," she promised, snapping on the tiny light plugged into an outlet on the wall next to the bed. "And if you need me, I'm only one room away. All you have to do is call me, okay?"

"Okay."

"Good night, Clay." She brushed his red hair away from his forehead, then couldn't resist leaning over to kiss his cheek. "Sleep well."

Two little arms locked around her neck for a warm

hug. Soft lips touched her cheek. "Good night, Miss Emily."

Emily returned the hug, then left the room quickly, a massive lump in her throat.

Wade had accused her of casting a spell on the Davenport males.

It seemed to her that he had that situation all turned around.

SATURDAY MORNING dawned crisp, cool and beautiful. Because Clay said he liked them, Emily made pancakes for breakfast, light and thin, with maple syrup. She served him a small bowl of sliced fruit on the side, along with a big glass of milk.

"This is good," Clay said, attacking his plate. "Cecilia usually just makes cereal for breakfast. Sometimes we have French toast or oatmeal, but we don't have pancakes very often. I don't think Cecilia likes to make them."

"I've heard very nice things about Cecilia," Emily said, cutting into her own pancakes.

"She's cool. I don't think she likes Honoria very much, though. She wants to go back to Atlanta."

Emily hadn't meant to pry. She'd almost forgotten that children tended to answer offhand comments with more information than was absolutely necessary. Still, she felt badly that Cecilia wasn't happy in Honoria. The woman was probably lonely, feeling like a stranger in a strange town. Emily would have to ask Wade if he thought it would be a good idea to introduce her to some of the locals.

Of course, she wouldn't be here much longer, herself. Soon it would be Emily who would be the stranger in a strange town.

Would she be as homesick as Cecilia?

She shook that troublesome thought away. How many times must she remind herself that this move had been her own decision, one she'd made only after careful consideration? And one she would not regret, she told herself firmly.

"When do you think my daddy will be here?" Clay asked.

Emily put her own worries out of her mind. "I don't know. But I'm sure you and I can find something to keep us busy until he gets here."

"Can I go play on your tire swing?"

"Of course. As soon as you finish your breakfast."

The boy turned his attention quickly back to his meal.

IT WAS NEARLY THREE in the afternoon when Wade called. "I'm going to be late," he warned after making sure his son was safe and happy. "Very late, I'm afraid."

"It's not going well?" she asked, hearing the strain in his voice.

"No." His tone was grim. "Not at all well. I'm really sorry, Emily. If you have plans for the evening, I'll try to make other arrangements for Clay."

"I have no plans," she assured him. "Clay and I are having a wonderful time. He's just discovered my art supplies."

"The kid loves to cut and draw and color. You probably won't see him again for hours."

"I've found that to be true of most of the children

who visit me. They all seem to love a big stack of blank paper and a handful of markers."

"Clay certainly does. You're absolutely sure you don't mind keeping him the rest of the day?"

"Not at all. He's an angel."

Wade's laugh sounded a bit more relaxed. "Well, not always. He has his moments."

"What time do you think you'll be back?"

"The way it looks now, it's going to be close to ten o'clock. You'll probably want to put Clay to bed, and I'll just carry him to the car when I get there."

"He's welcome to spend another night if you want to wait and come back tomorrow."

"Thanks, but I'm ready to get home, myself. I've got a lot of work waiting for me."

"Okay. I'll see you later this evening."

"Right. If you'll put Clay on the phone, I'll explain the situation to him."

"Of course. Clay?"

The boy came running in response to her call. Emily handed him the phone, then stepped aside to give him a semblance of privacy.

She watched as he listened intently to whatever Wade was saying. She wondered how Clay would react to hearing that he would be with her for the rest of the day. She was relieved when he said offhandedly, "Okay, Daddy, you don't have to hurry. I'm having fun here."

Absurdly, Emily felt as though she'd just been given a prize. And all because Wade's son was happy being with her. Oh, she was definitely headed for trouble if she wasn't careful!

"'Bye, Daddy. Love you more," Clay said in a rush,

and then giggled at whatever Wade answered. And then he turned to hand the phone back to Emily. "He said he wants to talk to you again. May I go draw again now?"

"Of course." Emily took the phone as Clay dashed away. "Wade?"

"Yeah. Just wanted to tell you thanks again."

"Not necessary. Drive carefully this evening, okay? You'll be tired."

"Nice to know you're concerned about me." His answer was spoken flippantly, but something in his voice made Emily bite her lip. "See you tonight, Emily," he added, then disconnected.

Emily had a sinking feeling that she would be counting the hours even more eagerly than Clay.

What a fool she was.

IT WAS ALMOST ELEVEN when someone tapped lightly on Emily's front door. She'd been sitting in the quiet living room, reading and waiting for Wade's arrival. She set her book aside and hurried to open the door.

She'd left the porch light on for him. His face looked haggard in the soft glare.

"You're exhausted," she said, studying him compassionately.

He ran a hand through his already disheveled hair, the gesture a weary one. "Beat," he agreed. "I got all of a couple of hours' sleep last night."

"Did you get everything worked out?"

"I think so. The situation looked better when I left than when I arrived."

"Then at least your time wasn't wasted."

"That's something, anyway," he agreed.

She closed the door behind him. "Have you eaten?"

Wade made a face. "I had a sandwich for lunch. Haven't eaten since. I'll pick up drive-through on the way home."

"You'll do no such thing. I have a plate of leftovers from dinner in the refrigerator. All I have to do is pop it in the microwave. Clay's sound asleep, so there's no reason you can't relax a minute before you take him home."

He looked decidedly tempted. "Aren't you tired?"

She shook her head. "I can sleep late tomorrow. Come on into the kitchen. Do you want coffee, or is it too late for that?"

He followed close at her heels, peeling off his denim jacket. "Got any milk?"

"Yes."

"Then I'll take a glass of milk. How did things go this evening with Clay?"

"He wasn't a bit of trouble. You have a delightful little boy, Wade. You must enjoy him very much." She set the plate of leftovers in the microwave, pressed the start button, then turned to pour him a large glass of milk—the same beverage Clay had requested for dinner, she thought with a smile.

"He's my life," Wade answered simply...and touchingly.

The microwave's beeping saved Emily from having to try to speak around the sudden lump in her throat. She slid the warmed plate in front of Wade, along with a fork, knife and napkin.

"Hey, this looks great." Wade spent a moment admiring the arrangement of baked chicken, wild rice and mixed vegetables. "This is what you fed Clay for dinner?"

"Yes. He seemed to like it." Emily poured herself a small glass of milk and took a seat at the table opposite Wade.

"No kidding. No wonder he was in no hurry for me to get here." Wade scooped a forkful of food into his mouth, chewed, then swallowed before saying appreciatively, "Delicious."

She smiled. "You're just very hungry."

"No, really. Clay and I are very fond of Cecilia, and she's a wonder as a housekeeper, but her cooking skills are only adequate at best. We don't complain, of course, because she more than makes up for that lack in other ways. She's been really good to Clay."

"Clay's afraid that Cecilia isn't happy in Honoria. I was going to ask if you thought it would be okay if I introduce her to some people around town."

"You could try, I guess. Cecilia's shy. And she's homesick for Atlanta. She came with us because she didn't want to say goodbye to Clay, but I'm not sure it's going to work out. I thought if she could get involved with an active seniors' group it would help, but she hasn't shown much interest in meeting people."

Emily lifted an eyebrow in surprise. "A seniors' group?"

He nodded. "She's sixty-six. She'd already raised a couple of kids of her own when she came to work for me. She was widowed, and lonely because both her children have moved away—one lives in California, the other in England. A mutual acquaintance brought us together, and it has worked out very well until now."

For some reason, Emily had assumed the housekeeper was younger. No wonder the woman had been reluctant to start over at this point in her life. "What will you do if she retires? Will you look for another full-time housekeeper?"

Wade shook his head. "Probably not. Now that Clay's in school, I really only need someone in the afternoons, except during school breaks, of course. He and I can make do for ourselves when I'm home from work."

Emily wondered if Wade ever thought of remarrying. He was still a young man, only a year or two over thirty, at most. She hadn't heard of him dating anyone in town yet, but surely he needed more in his life than his son and his work. Was he still in mourning for his wife, five years after her death?

Not that it was any of her business, of course, she reminded herself hastily.

Wade cleaned his plate in record time. "That was really good," he repeated after swallowing the last bite.

"I have chocolate cake," she said enticingly, wondering if his sweet tooth was as well developed as Clay's. Clay had attacked his dessert with amusing enthusiasm. "Wouldn't you like just a small piece for dessert?"

"Chocolate cake?" Wade repeated, his eyes brightening. "With chocolate frosting?"

"At least an inch of chocolate frosting," she promised with a smile.

"Oh, man, I've gone from a hellish day to a heavenly evening."

"Does that mean yes, you want some cake?"

He grinned. "Yes, I want some cake."

"Help yourself to more milk if you like while I cut you a slice."

He filled his glass to the brim again. "I'll pay for this, but it'll be worth it," he murmured, sitting back down to greedily eye the generous serving of rich chocolate cake Emily had set in front of him. "Aren't you having any?"

"I had my dessert earlier, with Clay. I'd better resist having more tonight."

He gave her an assessing look that brought warmth to her cheeks. "You hardly have to worry about your figure," he said, wriggling his eyebrows in a mock leer.

A bit flustered, she reached quickly for her glass. "I...um...try to watch what I eat," she muttered.

To her relief, he let it go, turning his attention back to the dessert.

There wasn't a chocolate crumb left on his plate when he finished, nor a drop of milk left in his glass. He patted his flat stomach. "Worth every calorie," he declared.

Emily couldn't help looking at him in much the same way he'd looked at her earlier. Wade didn't need to count calories, either, she thought. She found his solid build very appealing. Just as she found everything about Wade Davenport appealing.

She rose quickly to carry her glass to the dishwasher. Wade followed with his own dishes, which he rinsed and stacked into the dishwasher with a casualness that spoke of experience. Apparently, Cecilia had her men well trained, since Clay had also matter-of-factly cleared away his own dishes.

She closed the dishwasher and turned, only to find

herself suddenly, unexpectedly, only inches away from Wade.

He didn't move.

"I—er—excuse me," she said, shifting to go around him.

He placed his hand on her arm and held her where she was. "I think you really have cast a spell over me, Emily McBride," he muttered, his eyes locked on her mouth with an expression that resembled the hunger he'd shown for his dinner earlier. "Why is it that I can't stop thinking about you?"

She supposed if she knew the answer to that, she would know why *she* couldn't stop thinking about *him*. "Wade—"

"I can't get you—or your taste—out of my mind. I want to kiss you again."

She moistened her lips, which were already tingling in anticipation. "I—I thought we agreed that wasn't a good idea."

"That doesn't make me stop wanting it."

She wanted it, too. So badly she was trembling. She suspected that he could feel the quivers running through her, and knew he would interpret them correctly. She'd never been very good at hiding her emotions.

"Wade—"

"Let me kiss you, Emily."

His voice was low, silky, enticing. And she simply couldn't help herself. With a sigh of surrender, she wrapped her arms around his neck and lifted her lips to his incredibly sexy mouth.

9

WADE LOCKED his arms around Emily and lifted her against him, so tightly she could hardly breathe, as his mouth crushed hers. She wouldn't have complained even if she had been capable of speech at that point.

His hands ran down her back to cup her bottom through her jeans and pull her even more tightly against him. Emily quickly confirmed that he was, indeed, a healthy male with healthy male urges.

Which only fueled her own long-denied urges.

His mouth was hot. Damp. Thorough. His heart pounded against her, pumping as frantically as her own.

The hunger mounted.

Somehow her fingers found their way into the hair at the back of his head. It was short, but soft, and it showed a slight tendency to curl around her fingertips. Her breasts were flattened against his broad chest. The heat of his body penetrated the layers of clothing between them. His thighs, as solid as tree trunks, pressed against hers. And she felt a liquid heat flood her body, from her curled toes to her frantically flushed cheeks.

He tore his mouth from hers to gasp for air. "Emily." His voice was as rough as sandpaper. It grated pleasantly in her ears. "I've wanted you from the first time I saw you—even though I knew I should stay away from you. Every time I'm with you, I only want you more."

She knew it was pointless to deny that the attraction was mutual. Wade would see right through her.

She tried to remember why this was such a bad idea, when it felt so very good. "It can't go anywhere, Wade. I'm leaving soon."

"I'm not asking for promises of forever," he replied gruffly. "Only a night or two, if that's all you have to give."

"People would talk."

He lifted an eyebrow. "Does that bother you?"

She shook her head, trying to shake the images of Sam Jennings and April Penny out of her mind. "I'm used to it. All the McBrides are," she added with a touch of bitterness. "And it doesn't matter to me any longer what the people of this town say about me or my family. I'm leaving. But you're staying. And you're in a very public position. You don't know how vicious they can be."

"I'm not sure you're being fair. Most of the people I've met in this town have been very nice."

"Most of them are," she agreed. "But the ones who aren't so nice seem to be the most vocal."

Wade's eyes were entirely too perceptive as they studied her face. "You've been badly hurt."

"Yes," she answered candidly. "But I'm not going to let them hurt me any more."

"You're running."

"I'm leaving," she corrected him, a bit piqued by his choice of words. "Because I want to, not because anyone is making me. And that's why I think it's better if you and I don't let this go any further. There's no point to it."

"That's the reason you keep giving." He sounded openly skeptical.

"What other reason could there be?" she asked, lifting her chin.

"Maybe you're afraid that I could tempt you to stay."

Her heart tripped. "That's ridiculous," she said, trying to pull herself out of his arms. "And conceited," she added.

He didn't release her. "Maybe. But then, again, maybe I'm right."

He kissed her again, his hands sliding up her sides, pressing against the outsides of her breasts, making her shudder with wanting. She came all too close to melting against him, begging him to do whatever he could to tempt her to stay.

With a massive effort, she tore her mouth from beneath his, planted both hands against his chest and gave a slight push. It was like trying to move a granite wall. "You aren't right," she insisted, her voice hardly recognizable even to her. "Nothing is going to stop me from leaving this town and finding a life somewhere else."

He brushed his fingers over her swollen lips. "You're sure about that?"

"Ab—" She stopped to clear her voice. "Absolutely."

"Then there's no reason we shouldn't spend a little time together before you go, is there? Nothing at all for you to be nervous about."

The slightest hint of a taunt in his voice made her

eyes narrow. "I'm not nervous about spending time with you," she corrected him firmly. "I was only trying to spare you from being the topic of small-town gossip."

"Oh. So you were turning me down for my own sake." This time he made no effort to hide his disbelief. "How very thoughtful of you."

She shoved again, and this time he let her go. She planted her fists on her hips, knowing she looked anything but intimidating with her hair all tumbled and her mouth still damp from his kisses. But she tried to speak coolly, anyway. "Okay, fine. If you don't care what the people around here say about you, then why should I?"

"Exactly. So you'll go out with me?"

She shrugged. "Why not? I have some spare time in the next week or so, and I find you rather amusing."

If she'd been trying to annoy him—and she had— she failed. Wade laughed. "I find you rather amusing, too, Emily McBride," he murmured, and brushed a kiss across the tip of her nose. "I'll call you."

"Fine."

Only after Wade had left, carrying his sleeping son in his arms, did it occur to Emily that she had just been manipulated by an expert.

What had she been thinking? Hadn't she been determined not to get involved with Wade Davenport? And now she'd agreed to go out with him. And if she backed out now, he would be convinced it was because she was afraid of falling in love with him, or some such nonsense.

She gulped, wondering nervously just how nonsensical that idea really was.

"WHAT'S THIS I HEAR about you dating Emily Mc-Bride?" Martha Godwin demanded of Wade on Monday afternoon. She had come to his office on the pretext of complaining about the noise her neighbor's teenagers made in the afternoons after school, but Wade sensed that she had just admitted the real reason for her visit.

"What makes you think I'm dating Emily McBride?" Wade asked mildly, unwrapping a stick of gum—only because he knew it annoyed Martha when he chewed it.

She eyed him suspiciously. "You haven't been on a date with her?"

"No," he replied, though that was only a technicality now that he'd finally finagled a tentative agreement out of Emily. But it was the truth. They hadn't officially been on a date as of yet. And it was none of Martha Godwin's business that Wade intended to remedy that situation as soon as possible.

"I also heard that you're buying her house."

"That part is true," he acknowledged. "I've made an offer, and the deal is underway. It takes a while to get all the paperwork filed."

"Where's she going to live when you move into her place?"

"I don't know. I'm not privy to her personal business."

But Martha Godwin wouldn't have recognized a hint if it walked up and pinched her broad butt, he thought when she only nodded and said, "Well, it wouldn't be so bad if you *were* to ask her out. Emily's a nice girl. Past time she settled down with a husband and family of her own. I guess that's why she had to sell the house and land? Too much for her to take care of by herself? Not that her father was ever any help to her. Of course, I heard his medical bills ran up pretty high, too. Guess she needed the money from the sale of the place."

Wade remained silent.

"Yes, I think you and Emily would make a nice couple," Martha continued with a nod of her silvery head, as if the whole thing had been her idea from the beginning. "You need a mother for that little boy, and she needs a man to take care of her. You can bet she won't be getting any help from that no-account, murdering brother of hers, wherever he is. Just like his father, that boy was. Mean as a snake and a temper like a volcano. Josiah, Jr. was a thoroughly unpleasant man. His first wife died of pneumonia, and she didn't seem to want to fight very hard to live. And his second wife, the wildest young woman we've ever seen in these parts, ran off after being married to him less than five years. Maybe folks could've understood her leaving Josiah, but she shouldn't have run off with another woman's husband, leaving his family and her own little girl behind to grieve."

Wade could almost feel the blood trickling out of the side of his mouth as he bit his tongue to keep himself from responding to anything Martha Godwin had just said.

"Hmmph," she muttered, studying his face and apparently coming to the conclusion that he wasn't going to give her the satisfaction of gossiping with her. "Well, you see what you can do about those Smith kids, you hear? And what have you done about those break-ins around here lately? It's been going on for more than a month now, and as far as I can see, you and your officers haven't done a thing about them."

"The case is still under investigation, Mrs. Godwin. Now, if you'll excuse me, I have work to do."

It usually took a bit more effort than that to get rid of her, but maybe she sensed that she'd pushed Wade far enough that afternoon. With another *hmmph* and a shake of her head, she marched out of his office, closing the door behind her with a firm snap. Wade resisted the temptation to throw something at that same door in sheer exasperation.

Wow. Emily hadn't been kidding about the gossip around here. If Martha could be that brazen to Wade's face, heaven only knew what she'd been saying behind his back.

But he told himself he wasn't going to worry about that. It was none of the town's business what relationship—if any—he had with Emily McBride.

He remembered Emily's airy statement that she wouldn't have to worry about the gossip because she wouldn't be around much longer. And he scowled—as he always did when he thought of Emily moving away.

If it was up to him, she wouldn't be going anywhere—at least, not anytime soon.

Problem was, Emily didn't think he had anything at all to say about her plans. Well, he was just going to have to see what he could do about changing her mind.

EMILY HAD a meeting Monday evening that lasted until nearly nine o'clock. As she drove home, tired from a day of work and socializing—and from a long night of thinking about Wade's kisses—she told herself that her community-service days were almost over. At least in Honoria.

In the new life she envisioned for herself, she might occasionally get involved in projects that served society, but it would be at her own discretion, she privately vowed. When *she* felt like it. She would no longer be at the beck and call of people who had gotten all too accustomed to counting on her.

She stretched as she climbed out of her car. It had been a very long day. She was looking forward to getting inside, where she would make herself a cup of hot tea and snuggle onto the sofa to read or watch TV— and try not to think about Wade.

With her thoughts centered on the sexy chief of police, she shook her mother's heavy bracelet back on her arm to keep it out of the way as she pushed her key into the lock of her front door. Nothing seemed in the least out of the ordinary to her—until she stepped into her house. Suddenly, she had a sense that something was wrong. Hadn't she left a lamp on to greet her when she arrived? *What...?*

A blow on the back of her head made her stagger, her ears ringing, her stomach lurching in response to the violent pain. And then something hit her again. She plunged to the floor and into a darkness that echoed with terror.

WADE HAD TOLD HIMSELF he wasn't going to stop by Emily's house that evening. Wasn't even going to call her. He wanted to give her a little time to think about what had happened between them in her kitchen. And he didn't want to appear too eager...after all, he had his pride to think of.

As he found himself turning into Emily's driveway, he came to the rueful conclusion that he had no pride— or self-control—when it came to Emily McBride.

He hadn't even made a conscious decision to drive to her house. He'd tucked his son into bed, and then, after telling Cecilia he'd be home later, he'd climbed into his Jeep and turned the key. He often went back to his office after Clay went to sleep; he liked being there in the evenings when there were fewer interruptions and he could plow his way through the piles of paperwork that always seemed to accumulate on his desk.

But he hadn't gone to his office, or even steered the Jeep in that general direction. He had driven straight to Emily's, as if drawn by a force he simply couldn't resist. Which wasn't a bad way to describe his overall reaction to Emily since the first time he'd seen her.

He knew the minute he climbed out of his Jeep that something was wrong. Her car was parked in its usual place, but the house was dark. And the front door was standing open.

Instincts honed by years of police work kicked in, and Wade broke into a run. "Emily?"

He paused only a moment in the doorway. "Emily?" he yelled.

He thought he heard someone moan. He ran into the house, only to almost stumble over her where she lay on the living-room floor. Cursing frantically beneath his breath, he groped for a light switch. Light finally flooded the room.

Emily lay tumbled on the carpet, her golden curls tangled, her face pale, her long skirt twisted around her legs. The living room had been trashed—drawers opened, books strewn, cushions tossed on the floor. A small table was overturned next to Emily, the knick-knacks that had been displayed on it scattered around her.

His heart stopping, Wade went down on one knee beside her. "Emily? Honey?"

To his relief, her eyelids fluttered, then opened, squinting against the light.

Very carefully, his hand not quite steady, he brushed her hair back from her face. The darkening lump on her forehead caused him concern, as did the blood trickling from a small cut in the center of it. She must have hit the table as she'd fallen.

She focused on him intently, as though trying to remember his name. "Wade?" she said after a moment, her voice hoarse.

"Yes. Can you see me clearly?"

"I was thinking of you," she murmured, still drifting. "When I walked in..."

He ran his hands over her arms and legs, then carefully probed the back of her head. The large lump he found there both appalled and infuriated him.

Someone had hit her.

"I'm going to call for an ambulance," he said, trying to keep his voice calm. "You lie still."

"No." Her fingers curled around his arm with unexpected strength, detaining him when he would have risen. "No ambulance. I'm okay."

"Emily, you took a nasty blow to the head. You're going to have it x-rayed, and I'm afraid I'm giving you no choice on that."

She sighed. "I'll go, but not in an ambulance. Please. You take me."

"All right," he agreed, hoping he was doing the right thing. "But let me call this in first."

"Someone was in my house. My things..."

"You must have interrupted another break-in. We'll find out exactly what's missing, if anything, after we make sure you're all right, okay?"

She started to nod, then bit back a groan and lifted a trembling hand to her forehead. "My head hurts."

"I know, honey. Just lie still and I'll be right back."

When he found out who did this, he thought as he punched buttons on her telephone, he'd better make sure that someone else made the arrest. He couldn't guarantee that he could control himself...and he wasn't going to risk losing a conviction because of a police-brutality charge.

A few minutes later, he hung up the phone and turned back to Emily, knowing that a patrol car was on the way. He'd explained that he would be leaving for the hospital and would return as soon as he'd made sure that Emily was all right.

Emily was sitting up, her head on her raised knees.

"I told you to lie still," he fussed, kneeling beside her again.

"It hurts too badly to be still."

"All right. Let's get you to the hospital."

He placed one arm behind her back, and slid the other beneath her knees.

Emily lifted her head, apparently making a massive effort to do so. "What are you doing?"

"I'm going to carry you."

"I can walk."

"You can't even hold your head upright. Be still."

She didn't seem to have the strength to argue with

him. Her head fell weakly onto his shoulder when he rose with her held securely in his arms. She felt light and heartbreakingly fragile as he carried her out to his Jeep. And he thought it would almost be worth risking a lawsuit if he could just get his hands on the scum who had hurt her.

EMILY WAS DIAGNOSED with a mild concussion. No skull fractures. After giving her something for pain, the doctor released her into Wade's care.

Wade wanted to take her to his house, where he and Cecilia could take care of her. Or, if she wasn't comfortable with that, he offered to drive her to her aunt and uncle's house.

Feeling stronger now that her pain had been brought down to a manageable level, Emily refused both options.

"I want to see what's missing from my house," she insisted.

"And who's going to stay with you tonight? You heard the doctor say you should have someone check on you a couple of times."

"I'll call Aunt Bobbie. She'll come," Emily replied confidently. "Please, Wade. Take me home."

For all that she'd been in such a hurry to move, she was suddenly almost overwhelmed with the desire to be in her own home.

She almost changed her mind when she walked into her living room, leaning on Wade's arm for support. She groaned, taking in the mess that someone had made. "Who could have done this?"

"That's what we're going to find out," Wade answered grimly. He glanced at one of the two uniformed officers who'd filled out a report on the break-in. "What have you found, Marley?"

"The back door into the kitchen was kicked in. The bedroom has been trashed. Drawers all through the house ransacked—probably looking for cash. A jewelry box was overturned on the bed. Some costume pieces scattered around. If there was anything valuable in it, it's probably gone. Maybe Ms. McBride can tell us. A TV and a VCR are stacked on the bedroom floor. The perps must have bolted without taking everything when Ms. McBride walked in on them."

"Did you have valuable jewelry or cash around the house?" Wade asked Emily, who had been listening intently to everything Officer Marley had said.

"I had a little cash in a drawer of the writing desk in my bedroom. Not much, less than a hundred dollars. And I don't really have any valuable jewelry. Just my diamond-stud earrings, and I'm wearing them. And my mother's..."

She glanced down at her arm and felt her voice catch in her throat.

"Your mother's...?" Wade prodded gently.

"My mother's gold bracelet," she whispered.

"It was in your jewelry box?"

"It was on my arm."

There was a moment of silence as everyone suddenly realized that whoever had knocked Emily down had paused to take the bracelet from her arm before running away. Emily watched as Wade's face, which had already been hard with anger, darkened even further.

She wouldn't want to cross him when he looked like this, she realized.

She hadn't really seen him in cop mode before. Even when he'd questioned her about the embezzlement of Sam Jennings's office funds, he'd seemed mild mannered and self-possessed.

He looked downright dangerous now.

A few minutes later, Wade walked the two uniformed officers outside while Emily leaned back against the cushions of her sofa, her eyes closed, her headache now settled into a persistent, dull throb. She was having trouble thinking clearly; she blamed the painkillers the hospital staff had pumped into her, though she knew that shock was a good part of it. Never in her wildest dreams had she ever imagined that she would be attacked in her own home, here in the little town where she'd spent her entire life feeling utterly safe, if increasingly restless.

She wondered if she would ever feel so naively sheltered again.

"Emily? Honey, are you okay?"

She opened her eyes to find Wade bending over her, not looking dangerous now, but touchingly concerned. "I'm okay," she said. "Just tired."

"I'll call your aunt."

"Wait." She spoke without even stopping to think. "Not yet."

Wade hesitated. "What is it?"

"I know you probably have other places to be, but...would you sit with me, just for a minute?" she asked apologetically. "I need just a little time to recuperate before Aunt Bobbie comes to fuss over me."

"There's nowhere else I need to be right now," Wade assured her, taking a seat beside her on the sofa. "Can I get you anything? Something to drink?"

"No, thank you." She only wanted to sit with him for a little while, to know he was there. And that he cared.

What she really needed, she thought with a lump in her throat, was to be held. But that was something she couldn't bring herself to ask him.

She didn't have to ask. Wade reached out and pulled her into his arms, tucking her wounded head gently into his shoulder. His warmth enveloped her, wrapping her in a safe, snug cocoon.

She hadn't intended to cry. At least, not in front of anyone. She'd told herself she had more courage, more dignity than that. After all, she was lucky. She hadn't been badly harmed. Nothing of great value had been taken....

She buried her face in Wade's throat and felt the tears spill out, wetting his skin and her own.

Wade held her closer, murmuring something comforting and incoherent, except for the endearments scattered among the reassurances.

"My mother's bracelet," she said brokenly, naming the only thing that had been taken that truly mattered to her. "It was all I had of her."

"I wish I could promise that I'll get it back for you," he murmured against her hair. "But all I can promise is that I'll try."

Without drawing away from him, she lifted one hand to swipe at her face. "It shouldn't have mattered so much to me. I don't even remember her. She abandoned me when I wasn't quite two. I should hate her."

"But you don't."

"I tried, when I was growing up without a mother. Especially after Lucas left, and there was no one left but Dad and me."

"Was your father good to you, Emily?"

The careful way he phrased the question told Emily that Wade had heard something about Josiah, Jr.

"He never hit me," she assured him. "He never touched me, actually. Not a hug. Not a word of praise or affection. Lucas gave me my hugs when I was little, and it was Lucas who helped me with my homework and fixed my broken toys and comforted me when I had bad dreams."

"How old were you when your brother left?"

"Almost thirteen. After that, I went to Aunt Bobbie when I needed affection."

"But you stayed with your father all those years, taking care of him."

She nodded, wondering how to make him understand. "He had no one else," she finally said simply. "He'd alienated so many people. His brother Jonas died years ago, and he'd never gotten along well with Uncle Caleb. Uncle Caleb helped out when Dad became bedridden, but Dad didn't like having him around much. He had nurses when I was at work, and I took care of him in the evenings. At the end, I thought...well, I thought maybe he would have liked to thank me," she said. "But he couldn't speak by then. Maybe I was just reading into his expression what I wanted to see there."

"Or maybe not. It's entirely possible that he felt deeply grateful for your loyalty, and just didn't know how to let you know."

"I'd like to think so."

He stroked her hair, his fingers tangling in her tumbled curls, easing over the tender lumps at the back of her head. They sat that way, in comfortable silence, for several long minutes, until Emily finally stirred and sighed.

"It's getting very late," she said. "I should probably call Aunt Bobbie. Though I think I'd be perfectly fine alone tonight."

Wade's expression turned stubborn. "You heard the doctor. He said you should have someone with you. To be honest, I'd like to be the one to stay and take care of you, but since the whole town would be talking about it tomorrow if I did, I'm calling your aunt."

She felt her face warm. "I haven't even thanked you for all you've done for me this evening. Nor asked if there was a reason that you stopped by."

He stroked a strand of hair away from her cheek, then cupped her face in his palm. "Do you remember what you said when I found you lying on the floor?"

She had a vague memory of lying there, of squinting into a sudden bright light and seeing Wade bending over her, his brown eyes dark with worry. "I...er..."

"You said you'd been thinking of me when you came inside."

Her cheeks grew hotter. "I did?"

"Yes. And that was why I stopped by...because I'd been thinking of you, too. I seem to think about you all the time, as a matter of fact."

Emily moistened her lips, her face only inches from Wade's. "Do you?"

"Yes. All the time."

He leaned his head over, brushed his lips across hers as tenderly as if he thought she might shatter. But Emily wasn't feeling quite so fragile now. She reached up with both hands to hold his head to hers, deepening the kiss on her own.

Wade didn't hesitate to follow her lead. By the time the kiss ended, Emily's head was spinning, and it had nothing to do with her concussion.

"Tell me again why I'm leaving you tonight," Wade muttered.

She couldn't quite remember. "Because you have other things to do?"

"Nothing could be more important than this." He kissed her again.

"Because..." She couldn't seem to think of a reason, either, as he brushed his lips across hers once more.

"Because you need your rest," he said with a reluctant grimace. "And because we don't want to give the town gossips anything more to speculate about. What's your aunt's number? I'll go call her."

"Don't frighten her," Emily warned after reciting the number. "Make sure she understands I wasn't badly injured."

He nodded, then leaned over to kiss her one more time. "One night soon," he said when he finally drew away, "I'm not going to be leaving."

10

EMILY TOOK TUESDAY off work. Her headache was gone—or had at least subsided to an occasional twinge—but she was still bruised and sore, and she didn't quite feel up to facing her co-workers' sympathy and questions. Though they seemed inclined to stay all day to fuss over her, she finally persuaded her aunt and uncle to leave sometime late in the morning, promising to call them if she needed anything at all.

Her uncle had installed a new lock on the kitchen door and repaired the damage that had been done to it by the intruders. Her aunt had cleaned the house from top to bottom, making sure everything was back in its proper place. They left reluctantly, insisting that Emily lock up securely behind them.

It was a relief to be alone again, she thought as she heard them drive away. As much as she loved her aunt and uncle, and as much as she appreciated their loving concern, their constant hovering had begun to get on her nerves.

The telephone started ringing before noon, and didn't stop all day. It seemed that everyone in town wanted to inquire personally about Emily's well-being, and to ask for all the juicy details. Honoria hadn't seen so much excitement in years, she thought wryly, hanging up the phone after yet another call.

But she was surprised—and more than a little touched—that several callers had asked if there was anything they could do for her. Even Martha Godwin had wanted to know if there was anything she could bring Emily—and she apparently wasn't talking about her dog. What a refreshing change that was!

The telephone rang again beneath her hand. With a smothered sigh, she lifted it, thinking she really should put the answering machine on for a while to give her a chance to rest her ears. "Hello?"

"I just talked to Mother. She told me what happened to you last night. Are you all right?"

Though the caller hadn't bothered to identify herself, Emily recognized her cousin's voice. "I'm fine, Tara. Really," she assured the only daughter of Caleb and Bobbie McBride. "I got hit on the head, and I have a mild concussion, but there's no permanent damage. On the whole, it could have been much worse."

"I can't even bear to think about what might have happened." Tara seemed to shudder as she spoke. "Mother said you apparently interrupted the thieves before they could get away with much."

Emily thought fleetingly of her mother's bracelet, but she couldn't talk about that now. Not if she wanted to keep up the stiff-upper-lip facade she'd maintained for everyone else. "We believe that's what happened. He—or they—only took a few things they could stash in their pockets. We don't know if one person or more were involved."

"Dad seems to have some concerns about the new police chief. He said there were never so many break-ins before, and that no progress seems to have been made in solving them. Apparently, people in town are talking, beginning to wonder if they hired the right guy for the job."

Emily immediately grew defensive on Wade's behalf. "That's hardly fair. Wade's doing everything he can with the limited resources Honoria provides him. He's even asked for help from the state police. He's working long hours on these robberies, Tara, and I don't think anyone else could do any more toward solving them than he has."

Tara's voice held an undercurrent of amusement when she replied. "Mother told me you wouldn't like it if you heard what Dad had said. She said you and the police chief are...um...close friends."

"That's exactly what we are," Emily replied firmly. "Friends."

"I would certainly like to meet this Wade Davenport. Why don't you bring him to my wedding?"

"I'm sure Wade has plans to be with his own family on Thanksgiving weekend," Emily replied a bit stiffly.

"Mother told me he's a widower with a son. She said he's not too hard on the eyes, either."

Emily abruptly changed the subject. "Speaking of your wedding, how are the plans coming along?"

Tara chuckled at the obvious ploy. "Everything's going well. I can't wait to see you all in a few weeks. I was serious about you bringing a guest...and, by the way, children are welcome, too, if your date happens to have one."

"Tara, did you call to ask about my welfare or to harass me?" Emily asked in exasperation.

Tara laughed. "Both."

"Well, I'm fine and you've succeeded. So, if there's nothing else..."

"Okay, I can take a hint. I have to get back to work, anyway. I'll see you soon. And I'm really glad you're all right, Emily. I was so scared when I heard what happened."

Reassuring Tara again that no lasting harm had been done—no physical harm, anyway—and thanking her for her sincere concern, Emily finally hung up the phone.

It wasn't long afterward that her cousin Savannah called, having also heard the news. The conversation was similar to the one Emily had had with Tara. Savannah, too, required several reassurances that Emily wasn't seriously injured. And she expressed her horror that something so terrible had happened within the security of Emily's own home. It seemed that the whole family was having to change their perception of Honoria as a safe, sheltered, secluded place that big-city crime couldn't touch.

Savannah raved for a few minutes about her happiness with her new husband, renowned author and screenwriter Christopher Pace, and about how well her twin teenagers were adjusting to their terrific stepfather. And then she, too, mentioned that she'd heard Emily was involved with Honoria's new chief of police.

Swallowing a groan, Emily repeated that she and Wade were just friends, that there was nothing serious between them, that she had no intention of entering into a lasting relationship with the man. Savannah didn't seem to believe Emily's protestations any more than Tara had.

As Emily hung up the phone after Savannah's call, she reflected on how ironic it was that even her long-distance relatives had decided that she and Wade were meant for each other. Why couldn't they all understand that she wasn't looking to get permanently involved with *anyone?*

Not even a man as undeniably special as Wade Davenport,

WADE NEEDED some time to himself late Tuesday afternoon. It had been a hectic morning following a stressful night. Everyone wanted to know when he was going to solve the series of break-ins that had been plaguing their town—as if he and his staff weren't doing all they could.

He took a break at midafternoon to slip into a coffee shop close to his office and take refuge in a high-backed booth that offered him the first semblance of privacy he'd had all day. Nursing a cup of coffee and a slice of pie, he lingered as he thought about those increasingly frustrating robberies.

He had some possible suspects in mind—the O'Brien boy and his rebellious crowd of followers high among them. But there wasn't enough evidence to even think about making an arrest.

He was still shaken from finding Emily lying on the floor of her living room, though he'd done his best to conceal his emotions from everyone else. He could still remember the sheer terror that had flashed through him when he had seen the blood on her forehead, the deathly pallor of her skin. The strength of his reaction to that moment—and the distress the memory still brought him—only proved that his feelings for Emily weren't casual ones. That they never had been.

The public pressure on his department had been bad

enough before the attack on Emily happened, but now the townspeople had begun to panic. Martha Godwin had been standing at the door of Wade's office even before he arrived that morning, just to add her two cents' worth. She'd stayed until Wade had wondered if he was going to have to have her escorted away. Half an hour later, one of the two full-time reporters from the Honoria *Gazette* had called, demanding to know why Wade hadn't been more visible in his pursuit of the criminals who were, as he put it, "terrorizing their town and brazenly attacking innocent women in their own homes."

Emily had always implied to Wade that the locals didn't think much of her or her family. It certainly didn't seem that way to him, judging from the number of people who'd expressed concern about Emily's welfare. As far as Wade could tell, most of the Honoria's townspeople were quite fond of Emily. He couldn't imagine where she'd gotten a different impression.

It was the sound of Emily's name that drew Wade's attention toward a conversation going on in the booth behind him. Knowing the speakers couldn't see him, he listened as someone continued, "It's just a miracle she wasn't raped or killed."

Wade winced, having spent some uncomfortable hours during the night visualizing both of those horrifying possibilities.

"If I hear someone say 'poor Emily' one more time today, I just might be sick," another woman said scornfully. "I didn't know being hit on the head qualified a person for instant sainthood, or I might have tried it myself."

"Oh, April, you just don't like anyone in the Mc-Bride family," the first woman said.

April. Wade thought back to the fall festival, remembering the unpleasant food fight between the winner of the baking contest and the runner-up—April Penny. The woman who'd accused Emily of unfair judging.

"Can you blame me?" April retorted. "After all the vicious things the McBrides said about my poor brother when he refused to take responsibility for Savannah's bastard twins? Vince swore he hadn't fathered those kids, but the McBrides were determined to trap him. If his friends on the football team hadn't backed him up about Savannah's promiscuity, the McBrides might have permanently ruined Vince's reputation in this town. Now Savannah's married that rich, famous writer and they've got more money than God, and poor Vince is working his fingers off selling cars for a living. There's nothing fair about that, if you ask me."

"I did hear that Savannah got around some," the other woman admitted. "But Emily seems nice enough."

April snorted. "She's no better than her cousin. Everyone knows she's sleeping with the new police chief. Why else would he have been driving over to her house at nearly ten o'clock at night? What kind of example is that to set for his poor little boy? And you haven't been around long enough to know this, but I heard plenty about it when I was growing up—Emily's mother was the town whore. Slept with half the men in town, then ran off with a married one. He left his poor wife with two young children to raise on her own."

"That's terrible."

"And that's not all. Emily's brother is a cold-blooded murderer. He killed Roger Jennings—the son of the man his stepmother ran off with. Roger and Lucas used to fight all the time, and when Roger was killed, everyone knew Lucas did it, though no one could ever prove it. Especially with that silly Lizzie Carpenter swearing he'd spent the entire night with her—though most people thought that was just wishful thinking on her part."

"I'm still not sure you're being entirely fair to Emily. I haven't heard anything bad about her the whole time I've been in Honoria. Everyone seems to like her okay."

"If you ask me, she's no better than the rest of them. Sam Jennings hinted to me that she was caught in something shady at the bank, but she got off because the police chief had the hots for her. Guess we know how she repaid him?"

Wade had had enough. He set his coffee mug down with a thump and pushed himself out of his booth. His actions drew the attention of the gossips who'd been sitting behind him. At the sight of him, April Penny's face drained of color.

"Ladies," he drawled, his tone as cold as ice.

A touch of defiance returned to April's face. "Chief," she replied, just as coldly.

The other woman wasn't as quick to recover. She stammered a greeting that was mostly incoherent.

Several different put-downs lodged in Wade's throat. He considered and rejected all of them. After just standing there for a moment, looking at the women with narrowed, angry eyes, he decided his most prudent course would be to simply turn and walk away. He left a painful silence behind him, and knew that April Penny was well aware of his disdain for her.

He only wished he knew some way to make sure the woman never spoke Emily's name again.

EMILY WASN'T surprised when her doorbell rang late that evening. She'd been expecting it.

She started to open the door, then paused to first look out the window to make sure of her caller's identity. It wasn't something she'd been in the habit of doing before, but that old, comfortable sense of security had been forever shattered last night.

Confirming her guess that Wade was on the other side of her door, she ran a quick hand over her hair and let him in.

He studied the purple lump, still visible on her forehead, where she'd hit the small table as she'd fallen. "Still sore?" he asked.

"A little."

"How about the back of your head?"

"A little more sore," she admitted. "But on the whole, I'm fine. I'm going back to work tomorrow."

He held out a manila envelope. "I brought you something from Clay."

Emily frowned as she took it. "You didn't tell him what happened, did you?"

"I didn't have to," Wade answered grimly. "The kids at school took care of that. I reassured him that you're okay, and that I'm going to catch the crooks and put them in jail. That's a promise I intend to keep."

With misty eyes, Emily studied the drawing Clay had sent her. The boy had drawn a picture of himself holding a huge bouquet of multicolored flowers. In careful lettering at the bottom of the page, he had written, "Miss Emily, I'm sorry your head got hurt. Love, Clay."

She touched a fingertip to the funny little face in the child's drawing. "I think I'm in love with your son, Wade," she said, trying to speak lightly.

"Well, that's half the battle won," he muttered, and pulled her into his arms.

His mouth came down on hers with a hunger that only seemed to have intensified since the last time he'd kissed her.

She told herself she should pull away. No matter how spectacularly he kissed. No matter how good he made her feel. This wasn't wise. It couldn't last.

But, oh, how she wanted it to go on.

She wrapped an arm around his neck—only to steady herself, she decided, knowing a mental lie when she heard one.

Her mouth opened beneath his—but only because his probing tongue gave her little choice, she thought sheepishly.

And then she returned his kiss with a greed of her own—but only because she thought she'd die of wanting if she didn't, she admitted in surrender.

Maybe it was the attraction that had been building between them from the first. Or maybe it had something to do with the events of the past few days. But she didn't want to be reasonable and cautious and sensible now. She wanted Wade. She needed him...if only for tonight.

"Your head..." he murmured, drawing back only an inch or so.

"Is spinning," she admitted. "But it has nothing to do with my injuries."

"Emily, I..." He grimaced, as though he wasn't sure what to say.

Emily had no difficulty forming the words. "I want you, too, Wade."

It would have been pointless to lie. She had no doubt that he would have seen right through her.

His eyes glittered as he drew her closer again. "Are you sure?"

"I'm sure I want you. I'm not at all sure it's wise," she said.

"And are you always wise, Emily McBride?" he asked, his lips moving teasingly against hers.

She almost groaned with the longing that welled inside her. "I've always tried to be," she whispered. "But tonight..."

He kissed her lingeringly. "Tonight?" he prodded.

"Tonight I don't want to be wise," she murmured, drawing his mouth back to hers.

If she was going to start having all those adventures she'd dreamed of, she might as well begin tonight, she thought recklessly. And she could hardly imagine anything more exciting than making love with Wade Davenport.

Without allowing herself to think about it any longer, she led him to the bedroom she would always consider her own.

She had left a small lamp burning beside her bed. It provided all the illumination they needed as they turned to each other with searching eyes. Emily tried to gauge Wade's emotions from his expression.

Could this decision possibly be as momentous for

him as it was for her? Or was this something that Wade took more for granted? Something he did far more casually than Emily ever had?

He cupped her face gently in his hands, and she felt the faint tremors running through him. Looking into the warmth of his beautiful brown eyes, Emily realized that Wade wasn't taking this casually at all. In fact, he looked so serious, it made her nervous all over again.

She hoped he understood that tonight changed nothing as far as their future was concerned. So maybe she was a little in love with Wade—okay, maybe she'd tumbled head over heels, heart over head. But that didn't mean she intended to scrap all the plans she'd made. Not for a man she'd known less than two months.

Not for anyone.

And then Wade kissed her again, and she forgot about those plans for the future. Forgot the past. Forgot everything except this man, this moment.

His mouth was avid, his hands eager as the kiss turned from tender to frantic. Their clothing came off in layers, tossed heedlessly around the room as eagerness changed to impatience. They tumbled gracelessly onto the bed, laughing through kisses.

And then Wade slid his hand down Emily's body and the laughter changed to a gasp of delight.

That quickly, Wade's impatience was transformed. Suddenly, he seemed to have all the time in the world.

He began with her mouth. Devouring her lips. Sliding his tongue between her teeth to taste her. Kissing her until she wasn't sure if her euphoria was due to his skill or her lack of oxygen—and she didn't care.

He turned his meticulous attention to her right ear,

tracing the outer shell with the tip of his tongue, nibbling at her lobe. She shuddered. Until that moment, she'd been unaware of just how sensitive her ears could be.

And her throat. Just a brush of his fingertips from her jaw to the hollow made her tremble. When he followed that with a series of gently biting kisses from her throat to her breasts, she couldn't bite back a moan of pleasure.

By the time Wade had memorized every inch of her breasts and moved down to nuzzle her tummy, Emily had lost whatever semblance of rationality she might have retained.

It was only after paying close attention to every remaining inch of her body that Wade gave in to his own need. His movements growing urgent, he swiftly donned protection, and then returned to thrust deeply inside her. Emily welcomed him with a hunger that definitely equaled his.

As she cried Wade's name, Emily was aware of a touch of fear beneath the thrill. She'd wanted to believe that she could make love with Wade without falling so completely in love with him that nothing would ever be the same for her again.

She understood now what a fool she'd been.

"I WISH I COULD STAY all night...just holding you like this," Wade murmured after a lengthy period of recuperation.

Emily nestled her face more deeply into his bare shoulder and remained silent. She had mixed feelings about asking Wade to stay all night, sleeping in her bed. It would be wonderful, she had no doubt of that.

But she didn't want to risk growing even more attached to him than she was already. Not if she wanted to leave Honoria with her heart intact—more or less.

Wade answered himself with a faint sigh. "But I can't. Clay expects me to be there for breakfast, unless there's an emergency."

"You're a wonderful father, Wade," Emily said with a touch of wistfulness she couldn't quite conceal. "I'm sure Clay never doubts that he always comes first in your life. It's so obvious that you adore him."

Exactly the opposite of the relationship she'd had with her own father, she couldn't help thinking.

"I can hardly remember not being Clay's dad," Wade admitted.

"It must have been difficult for you at times, being both mother and father to Clay. He was so young when your wife died." It was the closest Emily had ever come to asking about Wade's late wife.

"He had just turned three."

"He doesn't remember her at all?" Again, Emily was putting herself in Clay's place, knowing exactly how it felt to have no memory of a mother's love.

"No. Not only because he was so young when she died, but because she wasn't a major part of his life while she was alive."

Startled by his words, Emily lifted her head to look at him. Wade's expression was solemn, his eyes shuttered. "What do you mean?"

"My wife and I married because she was pregnant with Clay," Wade answered flatly. "We'd been dating on what I naively considered a rather casual basis. I'd just finished the police academy. Kristi told me she was taking care of birth control. I was young enough and foolish enough to leave it up to her. It turned out she had lied. She had decided that marriage to me would give her the kind of security she'd never found in her dysfunctional home. What she discovered, instead, was that she didn't like being tied down to a husband or a child. We tried in our own ways to keep the marriage going, but it was effectively over even before she died while driving too fast on rain-slick roads."

Though he'd told her the story with little emotion, Emily sensed that Wade had suffered deeply during the past few years. "I'm sorry, Wade," she murmured, touching his face. "Because she died so young...and because your memories of your marriage aren't happier ones."

"Thank you. I'm sorry about both of those things, too."

Emily mulled over what he'd told her. After a pause, she asked carefully, "You never considered not marrying Kristi when she told you she was pregnant? Never questioned that the baby was yours?"

"I knew he was mine. And, no, I had no intention of allowing a child of mine to be born without my name. Old-fashioned of me, maybe, but that's the way I was raised."

"Too bad all men don't take that kind of responsibility for their actions," Emily said. "My cousin Savannah got pregnant with her twins when she was only seventeen. The father denied all responsibility and even got a bunch of his friends to lie that they had slept with Savannah. She swore to us that Vince had been the only one, and we believed her."

"Vince Hankins."

Wade said the name with a confidence that suggested he'd already heard the rumors. Emily wasn't surprised, considering the efficiency of the Honoria grapevine, and the lingering fascination with the McBride family in general. "Yes. The jerk. I wouldn't ever buy a car from him if I were you. Any guy who could lie as well as he did at seventeen is probably a master of the skill by now."

"I'll keep that in mind. I could never respect a man who didn't take responsibility for his own children."

"As it turned out, Savannah and the twins were better off without him, anyway. They're so happy with Kit—Christopher Pace, the writer. He and Savannah were recently married."

"I'm a big fan of his work."

"He's good, isn't he? I liked his futuristic thrillers even before Savannah met him. She was reluctant to get involved with him at first because of his celebrity. She'd been the subject of so much gossip here in Honoria that she developed a real obsession about her privacy. Of course, marriage to a man who makes his living writing bestselling books and blockbuster screenplays hardly guarantees that. But Kit quickly won her over."

"I'm glad things have worked out for her and the kids."

"So am I. I'm very close to both Savannah and Tara. They were like sisters to me growing up, and Tara's younger brothers were my playmates. I never got a chance to know my mother's family—most of her relatives moved away long ago, and my father never attempted to stay in touch with them. The McBrides have always been my only family, just as this has been the only home I've known."

"And yet you're still planning to leave at the end of the year."

She caught her breath. "Yes," she answered quietly after a moment. "I'm planning to leave."

Because she didn't want to think of leaving while lying in Wade's arms, she quickly changed the subject. "Are you hungry? I have about a dozen casseroles in the refrigerator. Several of my neighbors brought food when they heard what happened here last night—the standard small-town response to disaster," she added with a slight laugh. "As though green-bean casserole could make anything better."

"You have a lot of friends in this town, Emily. A lot of people who know just how special you are. The others—well, they simply don't matter," he said firmly.

She didn't know if he was referring to Sam Jennings and April Penny, or if he'd heard other slurs, but she appreciated his words. "Thank you. I try not to let the gossip bother me as much as it did Savannah, but sometimes it's hard to ignore. Especially when they talk about Lucas. Whatever you've heard, Wade, my brother didn't kill anyone. I will never believe otherwise."

"I would never judge a man's guilt without solid evidence," he assured her. "Or listen to gossip."

"Good for you. As you pointed out, the ones who say the nasty things about my family and me don't really matter."

"So why are you letting them run you out of town?"

The blunt question startled her into sitting upright. She made a hasty grab for the sheet to cover her bare breasts as she stared down at Wade, who still rested rumpled and relaxed against her pillows. "No one is running me out of town, Wade. I'm leaving by my own choice."

"Yeah, sure."

Stung by his obvious skepticism, she persisted. "I am. I need to know that I can make it on my own."

"I have no doubt of that. But I still think there's a very real possibility that you're acting on an impulse you'll regret. You aren't a footloose adventurer, Emily McBride, no matter how much you fantasize about being one. You'll probably enjoy your travels for a short while, but then you're going to think of home. And you're going to miss it."

She frowned. "Oh, you're psychic, are you?"

"No. Just a pretty fair judge of character. Comes with the job."

"Well, you're wrong this time. You're assuming that I was always happy in this house, Wade. I wasn't. My father and I weren't close. My mother hated this place so badly she left it—and me—behind. My brother couldn't wait to shake the dust of Honoria off his heels. What is there to hold me here now?"

"Your family. Your friends. Your memories, both good and bad, because they have made you who you are. And—I would like to think—me."

She bit her lip.

Wade studied her expression, then laughed with little humor. "Or maybe not."

"But, Wade, you and I aren't...we're only..."

"As of tonight, we're lovers. And that isn't something I take lightly these days...not since I became a father and had to start acting like an adult."

She twisted the sheet more tightly in her fingers, not knowing quite what to say. Had Wade really begun to think of a lasting relationship, even knowing that she didn't intend to stay? Had he really been so confident that he could change her mind?

And, if she really was so certain that leaving was the right thing to do, why was she so afraid that he might succeed?

Wade shoved a hand through his hair, and sat up. "Sometimes I've got really lousy timing," he muttered. "I'm sorry. I shouldn't have brought this up now. But I wanted you to know that tonight meant something to me, Emily. It wasn't just sex. And it wasn't casual. It was a hell of a lot more."

He caught the back of her neck with one hand and pulled her toward him for a quick, firm kiss. "I'm going to leave before I risk shoving the other foot into my mouth. But think about what I said, okay?"

She nodded, knowing she would have no choice but to ponder his words...and to wonder exactly how seriously he'd meant them.

Wade didn't linger after that. He dressed quickly, saying little more. Wrapping herself in a thick robe, Emily saw him to the door, where he paused only long enough to kiss her senseless again. And then he left her alone in the house that would soon be his.

She found herself suddenly wondering if it was too late to change her plans, even if she wanted to.

11

THOUGH HER BOSS and her aunt and uncle tried to talk her into taking the remainder of the week off, Emily went back to work Wednesday morning, still bruised and a bit sore, but desperately needing a distraction from her thoughts.

Her co-workers immediately surrounded her when she walked into the bank.

"Emily, are you all right?"

"Oh, Emily, we're so glad you're okay!"

"Are you sure you should be here today? Shouldn't you be resting?"

"Is there anything we can do for you?"

Again, she was struck by the novelty of having people offer to do favors for *her*. It was quite a turnaround for a compulsive pleaser to have people trying to please *her* for a change...and she wasn't sure how she felt about it. While it was nice, it also made her a bit uncomfortable. She simply wasn't accustomed to it.

It seemed that every customer that came into the bank that morning wanted to talk to her. To express sympathy. To ask questions. To subtly probe for information about her relationship with the chief of police.

By midafternoon, Emily had begun to wonder wearily if she should have stayed at home, after all.

She was crossing the bank lobby, having just delivered some paperwork to the account research department, when she suddenly heard a child's voice call her name. "Miss Emily! Miss Emily!"

She turned just in time to catch Clay as he launched himself at her.

Bending slightly to return the boy's hug, Emily noted that Wade was close on his son's heels. He gave her a rather sheepish smile over Clay's head. "I just picked him up from school. He wanted to see you," he explained.

"Is your head okay, Miss Emily?" Clay asked worriedly, studying the still vivid bruise on her forehead.

"Yes, I'm fine, sweetie," she assured him. Her smile felt a bit strained because she was so intensely aware of the attention they were receiving from her co-workers and the few customers in the bank.

"I was worried about you," Clay said. "My friends at school said bad guys knocked you out and took your stuff. But don't worry. My daddy's going to catch them and put them in jail."

"Yes, I know he will, if he can." Emily straightened to glance at Wade, hoping her expression wasn't as revealing to the curious onlookers as she feared. "Hello, Wade."

"How are you?" he asked, searching her face.

Reading many layers into the simple question, she tried to answer all of them with a firm, "I'm fine. Thank you for asking."

Clay tugged at the hem of the navy blazer she wore. "Miss Emily?"

"Yes, Clay?"

"My daddy said you can help me get my own bank account. I brought money. Twenty whole dollars," he added with a hint of awe. "My aunt sent it to me and I want to put it in the bank and save it for something big."

"Twenty whole dollars?" Emily acted suitably impressed. "Goodness, that's a lot of money. And, yes, I can certainly help you open your own account. Come with me."

Feeling as if she were running a gauntlet of approving smiles, Emily took Clay's hand and led him to her desk, with Wade following closely behind them.

This, she thought, was no way to convince the townspeople that there was nothing serious going on between her and the Davenport males.

WADE AND CLAY hadn't been out of the bank for five minutes before Emily's co-workers pounced on her.

"What a sweet little boy. And he's so obviously crazy about you."

"The chief is definitely interested, Emily. We saw the way he was looking at you."

"You're so good with that little boy, Emily. You'd be such a wonderful mother to him."

"That Wade Davenport's no fool," one of the older workers declared with a look of satisfaction. "He probably took one look at you and saw what a good wife and mother you would be."

Emily knew they weren't deliberately trying to be insulting. She was sure they considered their personal remarks to be complimentary, rather than intrusive. Maybe they even thought they were being encouraging, giving her support at a time when she needed it. After all, folks around here were accustomed to speaking their minds, making their neighbors' business their own, giving advice whether it was asked for or not. It was the way Honoria had functioned for decades, and a few more circumspect newcomers hadn't made any great headway in changing things, particularly among the older citizens.

They probably would have been surprised to learn that everything they said only frightened her more. It had worried her enough that Wade might be considering a permanent relationship based simply on attraction. But to think that part of his interest in her could be based on her qualifications as a stepmother for his son gave her an all-new basis for concern.

Her main reason behind selling her house and leaving Honoria had been that she'd grown tired of taking care of other people. She needed to be responsible for no one except herself for a while. She'd thought of having a family someday—she loved children. But she'd decided that she wanted to take time to tend to her own needs before she committed herself to a lifetime of tending to others.

Though her own parents had hardly served as examples, Emily had never doubted that when she had children of her own, she would dedicate herself to them fully. She'd watched her aunts and uncle with their children, had studied other happy families in town, and she knew how much love, time and effort it took to raise children successfully. She had no intention of deserting them when things became difficult, as her mother had. Nor would she hold herself so distant from them that they were never certain whether she even loved them, the way Emily's father had treated her.

Taking on a ready-made family at this point of her

life—well, she just didn't know if she could handle that.

She couldn't help thinking about her mother again as she drove home from work that evening. Nadine had married a widower with a young son. She'd been miserable, even after having a child of her own.

Granted, Wade was very different from Josiah Mc-Bride, Jr. More open and affectionate, less demanding and bitter. From gossip Emily had heard, she wasn't certain that Nadine had ever loved her husband, but had married him for his comfortable income—a motive that almost guaranteed disaster. But Emily had known Wade only six weeks, not nearly enough time to think about a permanent arrangement. And she had plans she couldn't simply change on a whim.

Where would she live if she remained here, now that she'd sold her house? How could she risk losing this one opportunity to get away, to travel and see the world, to be single, carefree, totally unfettered for the first time in her twenty-six years?

She entered her house warily, looking around for signs of entry before she walked in—another new experience for her. She wondered if she would ever come home confidently again...for the few remaining weeks she would live here.

Her phone rang. Closing and locking the door behind her, she hurried to answer it out of habit, though the answering machine was still on. "Hello?"

"Hi. Everything okay there?"

Everything except her pulse rate, which had suddenly skyrocketed in response to Wade's deep drawl. "Yes, it's fine."

"I'm still at the office. Came back after I dropped

Clay off at home. Thanks for your patience with him this afternoon, by the way. He was tickled pink to have his own bank account. Not to mention the football you gave him."

"Everyone who opens a new account with us this month gets one," she reminded him. "You'd be amazed how many people open accounts just for the giveaway."

"Yeah, well, I'm waiting for you to offer a free bass boat with every new account before I change banks."

She chuckled. "Hang on to that dream, pal."

"Not likely, huh?"

"Not unless the banking wars get a lot more competitive than they are now."

"Listen, I'm going to be finishing up here in a couple of hours. Why don't you and I go out for dinner afterward? You probably don't feel like cooking tonight, and I can call home and tell them I won't be eating there this evening."

She couldn't deny that she wanted to say yes. That she wanted to be with Wade again. That she wanted the evening to end exactly as it had the night before...in her bedroom.

A renewed surge of panic—triggered, perhaps, by the whispered echoes of her co-workers' remarks—made her say, instead, "Thanks, but not tonight. I'm really exhausted. I think I'll just have a sandwich or something and turn in early."

There was a brief pause, and then Wade spoke, obviously trying to sound understanding. "Maybe you shouldn't have gone back to work today."

"It wasn't so bad. Just tiring."

"Then why don't I bring something there? Chinese?

Barbecue? Chicken? Pizza? Anything's better than a cold sandwich, isn't it?"

"Thank you, Wade, but I'm really not too up to it tonight." *In many ways,* she could have added, but remained silent.

The pause was longer this time, heavier. Apparently, Wade sensed that there was more to her reluctance to see him than weariness. Just as obviously, he realized that this wasn't the right time to grill her about it.

"All right, then," he conceded after another moment. "Get some rest. I'll call you tomorrow."

"Good night, Wade."

"Emily, I...I'll miss you tonight," he said, sounding as if he'd abruptly changed what he'd originally intended to say.

"Good night, Wade," she repeated, not knowing what else to say. And then she hung up.

She stood for a long time with her hand on the telephone. Something drew her attention to the grouping of framed photographs on the table nearby. Moving as if in slow motion, she picked one up. Studied it. Touched a fingertip to the face of the boy in the picture.

Lucas, she thought, ignoring the stern-faced man and unhappy-looking woman holding a smiling baby girl. He hadn't been much older than Clay when this photograph was taken, but already he looked distant and angry. Only with Emily had he shown his tender side.

And then he'd left her without even saying goodbye.

How would he feel if he knew she was selling the house? Her father had left a will, leaving everything to her, making no mention of his only son. But Emily would have gladly shared what there was, if only she'd known how to contact her brother.

But she hadn't heard a word from him since he'd left. Maybe he'd never given her another thought.

Lucas had left Honoria and its pettiness behind without a backward glance. Who knew how many places he'd seen since? How many adventures he'd experienced?

She put the photograph down with a thump. Ignoring both weariness and hunger, she pushed herself into action.

By the time she fell into bed at midnight, so tired her entire body throbbed and her mind was too cloudy to think, she had accomplished a great deal.

WADE KNEW he should have called Emily before turning into her driveway at nine-thirty Thursday evening, but something had told him it was better to show up without warning, as he had before. He'd had a niggling suspicion that if he'd called, she'd have talked him out of seeing her again that evening, just as she had last night...and that was a chance he hadn't wanted to take.

He saw the curtain at the window beside the door flick when he rang the doorbell. Emily was checking the identity of her caller, something he hadn't noticed her do before the break-in. While he approved of her heightened sense of caution, he hated the reason behind it.

Maybe the news he had for her tonight would give her back a small portion of the confidence that had been stolen along with her mother's bracelet.

She opened the door partway. Apparently, she hadn't been home long. She was wearing a long, floral-print skirt with a soft pastel blue sweater that brought out the color of her eyes and made his hands itch to touch her. "Wade? I wasn't expecting you tonight."

"We caught them," he said, deciding direct confrontation was the most effective way to storm the emotional barriers she'd inexplicably erected between them since they'd made love.

The door opened a bit wider. "You caught them?"

He nodded. "An hour ago. They'd broken into the Gellmans' house out on Paradise Road. They knew the Gellmans were away this week, so they decided to help themselves to their stuff. One of my patrol cars was passing by checking on the place and the officers caught the kids before they were able to get away."

"Kids?" Emily repeated with a frown.

"The O'Brien boy and his cronies. I suspected him all along, but until tonight there wasn't enough evidence against them to follow up with a warrant. We've got him now. One of his buddies started crying and confessed to the entire string of break-ins...except for yours," he added a bit reluctantly. "They all swear they had nothing to do with the hit here."

Wade was tempted to tell her that the boys' insistence that they had nothing to do with the break-in and attack on Emily had been so fervent that he'd begun to wonder, himself, if they were telling the truth. The doubt had nagged at him ever since he'd left the kids in the lockup.

But Emily suddenly looked nervous again, and he had a need to reassure her. "Then who...?"

He put a hand on her arm. "I would bet they broke into your place, too. They don't want to admit it because there was a personal attack involved this time, and they know that's a more serious charge."

He wanted to believe it was true. And maybe it was. It was hard to imagine that there was more than one burglary ring operating in Honoria. And as far as he knew, there was no reason anyone would have targeted Emily specifically. She'd had nothing of real value taken, nothing that had been worth the risk of being caught in her home or charged with attacking her.

"Kevin O'Brien." Emily shook her head in disbelief. "I can't believe it. I know he's been in a lot of trouble, but I had no idea he would resort to something like this. It isn't even as if he needed money. His father is a very successful businessman. He owns O'Brien Lumber, you know."

"It wasn't for the money. It was for the meanness," Wade said grimly. "Kevin O'Brien is a prime example of a kid who's had too much given to him and too few limits set. He set up a burglary ring because he thought it was fun."

"Fun," Emily repeated, and he could see the memories of pain and fear reflected in her eyes. "He thought it was fun to terrorize his hometown? His neighbors?"

"He turned eighteen last month. He's being charged as an adult. We'll see how much 'fun' he finds in the justice system."

"I don't suppose you'll ever find my mother's bracelet."

The wistfulness in her voice made him want to promise her anything. But he was more realistic than that. "We'll try. But I'm afraid I can't guarantee anything."

"No, of course not. But thank you for trying."

Wade motioned toward the door she still held in a white-knuckled grip. "Are you going to invite me in?" he asked, abandoning both patience and etiquette.

He watched her throat move as she swallowed. Why was she suddenly so nervous of him? And should he take that to be a good sign or a bad one? "Yes, of course," she said after a moment, stepping aside. "Come in. I have some fresh coffee in the pot. Would you like a cup?"

He closed the door behind him, started to accept her offer, then fell silent when he noticed the condition of her living room.

The floor was covered with large cardboard boxes. They were all open, and he could see that many of them were at least partially filled with things that had once decorated her bookshelves and tables. "What have you been doing?"

She smoothed her hands down the sides of her long skirt. "I thought I'd better get started on my packing and sorting."

His first impulse was to dump the contents of every damn box in the middle of the floor and then personally return every item to the place it belonged. He shoved his hands in his pockets and tried to speak casually. "What's the big hurry? The lease on my house isn't up until the end of the year, another six weeks."

"Six weeks passes quickly," she answered with a slight shrug, not quite meeting his eyes. "Especially when I have a whole lifetime worth of stuff to go through. I'm going to have a big yard sale here at the beginning of December, I think. Whatever I decide to keep will be put in storage."

Wade's hands fisted in his pockets. "You're going to sell your things?"

She moistened her lips before she replied. "Well, obviously I won't need all these things when I have no place to store them. I'll probably settle into an apartment somewhere eventually, and I won't have room for a houseful of furniture and knickknacks."

"So you're still planning to run away." He spoke in a flat voice that showed little of the emotion he was trying to hold inside. "You're just going to take off and 'find yourself' somewhere. No commitments to anyone. No ties."

Her chin lifted in response to the implied criticism. "Yes, that's right," she said with a touch of defiance. "For once in my life, I'm going to be responsible for no one but myself. And if that sounds selfish...well, so be it. That's something else I've never had the freedom to be."

"Bull."

Her eyes narrowed. "Excuse me?"

"You have had every freedom to be selfish. Everything you've done since you were old enough to be out on your own has been by your own choice. You didn't have to stay and take care of your father. Your mother and brother didn't. You chose to accept that responsibility. You weren't forced at gunpoint to join every community-service organization in town, and to be active in them. That was something you did because you wanted to, because you liked the feeling you got from making a difference in your community. You haven't been a prisoner in this house, Emily, nor in this town."

"I never said I was a prisoner," she answered defensively.

"You've chosen to be involved because you're happier being involved. You enjoy doing things for people you care about. And your community means a lot to you. You're not going to be happy drifting around the country, alone and unattached."

"And just what makes you such an expert on what I'm like?" she demanded. "On what makes me happy?"

"I know you," he answered simply—and then risked everything. "I love you."

He heard her breath catch, saw her eyes widen. And he wondered why his words would cause her to react in sheer panic.

She shook her head and literally took a step back from him. "No, you don't."

He followed her, taking two steps forward. "Don't tell me what I feel."

Another step backward. "You hardly even know me."

Two more steps forward. "I know enough. I'm no inexperienced kid, Emily. I know the difference between love and lust or infatuation. I wasn't in love with my wife. I knew that when I married her. I tried to be, but it didn't happen. It happened with you."

She was backed up against a wall. She stood there with her hands in front of her, warding him off. "I don't want this," she whispered. "I never wanted it to go this far."

"If you really meant that, you never would have made love with me." He lifted a hand to her face, just brushing her flushed cheek with his fingertips. "Do you really think I couldn't tell what a serious decision that was for you?"

Her flush deepened. "It isn't something I take casually," she admitted.

"Neither do I."

"But," she added firmly, "I warned you even then that nothing had changed."

"And I didn't believe you even then," he replied gently. "Everything changed for me that night. And I think it did for you, too...if you'll just admit it."

She shook her head, her face moving against his hand. "No. I'm still leaving. I...I have to, Wade."

"Why? Because you've said you're going to? Because you've sold your house?"

"Because if I don't, I'll never know," she corrected him quietly.

She'd effectively silenced him with that one, he thought with a touch of resignation. He'd been involved in a relationship—in a marriage—with a woman who'd wanted to be somewhere else. Anywhere else. It had been miserable for both of them.

He didn't want to risk getting into a situation like that with Emily.

Though it wasn't immediately apparent at the moment, he'd like to think he'd learned something from the disaster of his marriage. But what kind of masochist was he, to keep getting involved with women who didn't want to stay with him?

He sighed and slipped his hands on either side of her face. Resting his forehead against hers, he murmured, "I won't try to hold you here. I couldn't if I wanted to, obviously. But if you change your mind, I'll be here. And if you leave, then find that you aren't as happy as you thought you would be, I'll still be here."

"I'm not asking you to wait for me. That's...hardly fair to you." Her voice was thick with emotion.

"I love you, Emily. That feeling won't just go away when you do."

He heard her breath catch again, in what might have been a swallowed sob. "Please, don't keep saying that."

"Not saying it won't make it any less true."

"Wade, I..."

He kissed her into silence, smothering her apologies and excuses beneath his lips. And her response gave him reason to hope that he wasn't wrong about her feelings for him, though he had no idea why it scared her so much to admit them.

He crowded her back against the wall, his body pressed into hers so that she would have no doubt that he wanted her. He felt her shudder of response, and knew that the passion that had flared between them only two nights ago had not cooled.

He was unable to resist sliding his right hand between them, cupping her left breast through the impossibly soft blue sweater. He rubbed his thumb over the nipple that hardened beneath his touch, just as it had hardened in his mouth the night they'd made love. And the way she shivered let him know that she remembered every moment of the magic they'd shared.

"Damn, but I want you again," he muttered into her mouth.

"I want you, too," she whispered, seemingly helpless to deny it. Her fingers were tangled in his shirt, clinging, holding him against her. "Oh, Wade."

He crushed her lips beneath his and thrust his tongue deeply into her mouth, needing one last taste of her before he left. She opened to him, welcoming him with a touching eagerness that was almost his undoing.

She was limp in his arms by the time he drew away. Very carefully, he set her away from him, making sure she had one hand on the wall behind her for support before he released her.

"I'd better go," he said gruffly. "Before I do something I'll regret."

Like beg you to love me.

She blinked, startled, looking as though she had abruptly crashed to earth. "You're...leaving?"

"I can't love you again and then just watch you walk away. I have a heart, Emily...and it will only take so much."

She bit her lip, her gaze sliding away from his. Wade hesitated a moment, aching with need for her, calling himself a fool, wishing she would say something to change his mind. And then calling himself a fool again.

He turned on his heel and headed for the door before he could change his own mind.

Emily followed him silently to the door. He couldn't resist kissing her one more time before he stepped outside. "Good night. Call if you need me, okay?"

She nodded, and started to close the door behind him. And then something made her pause. "Wade?"

He turned on the porch to face her, hope flaring. "Yes?"

"Some..." She stopped, cleared her throat and began again. "Some people are saying you're interested in me because of Clay. Because you think I'd be a good stepmother to him."

Hope turned to a hot surge of anger. Emily must

have seen the flare in his eyes, because she immediately looked twice as nervous as she had before. "I...er...just thought you'd want to know what people were saying," she said hastily.

"Not particularly," he answered a bit too evenly, trying to control his temper—which wasn't usually so difficult for him. "I think I've told you before that idle gossip doesn't concern me. Had you been the one to make that accusation, I might have gotten mad...or hurt. But since you and I both know that I'm quite capable of taking care of my son without anyone's help—yours included—then there's no reason for you to question my motives, is there?"

"I, um, just thought you'd want to know," she repeated. "Good night, Wade."

She closed the door abruptly in his face.

Wade stood there a moment, staring at that door with angry eyes, half-seriously considering kicking it in and carrying her to the bedroom, where he would make love to her until she had no choice but to tell him she loved him, too. Or better yet, maybe he'd track down everyone who'd ever hurt her, from her long-missing mother to her runaway brother to all the gossips in Honoria, and punch every damned one of them for leaving her so wary and suspicious.

But, instead, he punched his fist into his own hand, then turned, walked to his Jeep and drove away without looking back. Emily had to make her own decisions, he thought. He only hoped the choices she made would finally make her happy.

12

DURING THE NEXT TEN days, Emily didn't hear from Wade at all. Apparently, he had decided to give her what she'd asked for. Her freedom.

She could leave Honoria any time she wanted to now. Whatever details remained to be settled concerning the sale of the house could easily be handled by long distance or mail. She'd sorted and sifted through all her possessions, deciding what to sell, what to store, and what to have hauled away. She could have everything finished in less than a month, be on her way by Christmas.

Christmas. She couldn't even imagine spending the holiday without trimming a big tree in her living-room window. Or without arranging her cherished antique Santa Claus figures on the mantel above the fireplace.

But she couldn't—wouldn't—think that way, she told herself firmly. She would think, instead, of all the exotic places she could spend Christmas if she wanted to. The islands, maybe. Christmas in the tropics.

She picked up a creased and tattered travel brochure and studied the photograph on the cover. A couple walking hand in hand on a sandy beach, the sun setting colorfully behind them as waves lapped at their bare toes. She pictured herself walking on that same beach...alone. And suddenly, unexpectedly, her eyes filled with tears.

Bad idea. She set the brochure down hastily, blaming her sudden emotionalism on exhaustion.

She hadn't gotten much sleep during the past week and a half. Every time she closed her eyes, she'd hear Wade's voice saying, "I love you." And then the panic would set in, making her heart race, her stomach clench, her skin go clammy.

She had tried to analyze her fears, beginning with her feelings for Wade. Was it really love she felt for him? Or merely physical attraction? Or nothing more than affection, perhaps.

Memories flashed swiftly through her mind. Vivid pictures of Wade with his son. Wade smiling at her. Kissing her. Kneeling frantically beside her as she'd lain on the floor. Making love to her until she'd wept with joy.

Okay, she was in love with him. She couldn't deny it to herself, even if she never found the courage to admit it to Wade.

She told herself that part of the problem was his son. She wasn't ready to become responsible for someone else's child. The stress, the worries, the inevitable conflicts...why would she deliberately take those on?

But she loved that little boy. So much that her heart swelled painfully every time she pictured him running across the bank lobby, his eyes alight with the pleasure of seeing her, his arms open for a hug, his little voice crying out, "Miss Emily! Miss Emily!"

The thought of never seeing that child again hurt almost as badly as the thought of leaving Wade forever.

She remembered her co-workers' hints that Wade

was courting her only because he needed a mother for his son, and she wondered if that was what bothered her so badly. But she couldn't believe that, either. She'd seen the flare of fury in Wade's eyes when she'd mentioned what the others had said. The cool pride on his face when he'd reminded her that he could take care of his son very well on his own.

Of course he could. He'd been doing so for years. He didn't need Emily to become a mother for Clay. But for some reason, he'd convinced himself that he was in love with her.

And, as always when she thought of that declaration of love, she panicked. Spurred into frantic action, she continued the packing she'd been doing for the past two weeks, going room to room, closet to closet, drawer to drawer, refusing to dwell on memories or give in to sentiment.

She spent more hours poring over her travel brochures, trying to imagine herself in those exotic places. Trying not to imagine Wade there with her. She'd told herself she wanted to spend time alone...so why did the future suddenly seem so lonely? And what took more courage on her part—going off alone, or staying in the hometown where she'd spent so many years?

WHEN HER DOORBELL RANG on the Saturday afternoon before Thanksgiving, she answered with some trepidation, wondering if Wade had returned to try to change her mind again. And whether this time he would succeed, despite her undefinable fears.

It was with more disappointment than relief that she found Martha Godwin standing on the other side of her front door.

"Oh, hello, Martha. What can I do for you?" she asked, moving aside to invite the older woman in. *And please don't ask me to keep your dog again. Not now.*

Martha looked curiously around at the half-filled boxes on the living-room floor. "Hello, Emily. My, you've been busy."

"Yes. I'm getting ready to move out at the end of next month. There's a lot of work involved in packing up forty-odd years of household goods."

"I understand you're having a yard sale in a couple of weeks."

Emily nodded. "Obviously, I can't keep everything. I thought other people might like to have some of the things I no longer need."

"I see."

Still uncertain why Martha had called, Emily motioned toward the sofa. "Please sit down. Can I get you anything to drink?"

"No, thank you, dear. I just wanted to see how you've been," Martha replied, making herself comfortable.

Emily didn't believe it for a moment. Martha always had some ulterior motive. Gossip to spread or gather. A favor to ask. A complaint to make. Something. And Emily suspected she wasn't going to like this one.

"I've been well, Martha. Just busy."

"No lingering effects from that horrible attack? How is your poor head?"

"Fine. No lingering effects."

"I knew all along that Kevin O'Brien had something to do with those break-ins," Martha announced smugly. "If everyone had listened to me, the case would have been solved weeks earlier. Joe O'Brien is paying now for spoiling that boy rotten, and that's exactly what I told him when I saw him at the pharmacy last week."

"Oh, Martha, you didn't."

"I most certainly did. I told Joe years ago that he'd better take that boy in hand before he turned into a hardened criminal. But would he listen to me? No. I simply reminded him last week that he wouldn't have spoiled the child if he hadn't spared the rod."

Emily bit her tongue. She'd felt rather sorry for the O'Brien family, who'd been genuinely shocked by their son's behavior. Yes, they had spoiled Kevin, and they should have stepped in long ago to curb his growing wildness, but blaming them now served no purpose. It had been cruel of Martha to throw her uninvited advice in Joe's face at this point.

"And it's obvious that Kevin hasn't learned anything from the trouble he's in," Martha went on, oblivious of Emily's disapproval. "He's still being very defiant, and he still refuses to admit that he had anything to do with the vicious attack on you."

"Yes, well, it's up to the courts to deal with him now."

"Mmph. Most likely he'll get a slap on the wrist and be released to terrorize our town again."

Emily clasped her hands in her lap, wishing that Martha would just get to the point of her visit.

"At least for a little while we can feel safe in our homes again. Of course, we still have to deal with Wimpy Curtis wandering the streets at all hours. Why someone doesn't put that man in a home is beyond me."

"Wimpy is perfectly harmless and you know it, Martha," Emily was spurred into retorting. "He's just a sweet, befuddled old man who gets confused sometimes."

"He's getting worse. Why, yesterday he was walking down Main Street in his bathrobe and pajama bottoms at two in the afternoon. And then he spat, right on the public sidewalk. Not a foot from where I was standing."

Emily's head was beginning to ache—as it so often did when she spent much time with Martha.

"I went to Chief Davenport's office to file a complaint, but he wasn't there. Of course, he was home with that sick boy of his, and I understand he has to take care of the child, but who's supposed to be watching out for the citizens of Honoria while he's away, I want to know?"

Emily lifted her head sharply. "Clay's sick?"

Martha's left eyebrow shot upward. "Why, yes. Didn't you know?"

"I, um, haven't talked to Wade in a few days. What's wrong?"

"Flu. A bad case, from what I've heard. And of course, with that housekeeper of theirs moving back to Atlanta last week, that's left the poor chief to deal with the boy on his own. And Officer Montgomery told me that when she called to check on them yesterday, the chief didn't sound so good, himself."

Emily sprang to her feet without thinking. "You mean they're both ill? And Cecilia isn't there to help them?"

"Why, no. I just assumed you knew, dear. You and the chief seemed so close. Have you quarreled?"

If Martha was there to dig up the dirt on Emily and

Wade's relationship, she was destined for disappointment. Emily had no intention of discussing her personal business with the woman.

"You'll have to excuse me, Martha, but I have a great deal to do this afternoon," she said, moving purposefully toward the front door. "So, if there's nothing else I can do for you..."

"Actually, there is one little thing." Martha stood, but didn't move immediately toward the door. "You know those little cranberry-glass dessert dishes that belonged to your father's first wife? Were you planning to sell those, by any chance?"

"I—"

"Because if you were," Martha went on without waiting for Emily to answer, "I'd like to buy them from you. There's no need to put them into your sale. And the price I'm prepared to offer is quite reasonable, I assure you. The collector books would probably list them higher, if you've checked, but you know those prices are always inflated. You can trust me."

"I'm sorry, Martha. The cranberry glass isn't for sale." Emily opened the door.

"But, Emily, you said yourself you don't need all these things. And it isn't as if you have a sentimental attachment to them. They belonged to your father's first wife, not to any of your relatives."

"They aren't for sale, Martha." *And neither is anything else—at least, not to you,* Emily wanted to add.

"Well." Insulted, Martha lifted her nose and stalked out the door. It was the first time that Emily had ever refused her anything. Maybe the first time *anyone* had had the nerve to refuse her anything.

Hardly giving Martha another thought, Emily closed the door behind the incensed woman.

Clay was ill. Wade, too, perhaps. And the housekeeper had left them to fend for themselves.

Why hadn't Wade called?

She never stopped to consider how ironical it was that she was downright angry over his neglecting to call her for help, when she'd spent so much time complaining about people doing just that. She simply grabbed her purse and marched out the door, her movements every bit as royally offended as Martha's had been.

WADE LOOKED like hell. His brown hair appeared to have been styled with a hand mixer. There were purple hollows beneath his eyes and the tip of his nose was red. A flush of fever stained his unshaven cheeks. His shirt was wrinkled, half-buttoned, and hung untucked over his jeans. He just stood there, blinking at her.

Emily's first instinct was to put him straight to bed. Her second was to crawl in with him.

"Where's Clay?" she demanded, stepping past him.

"He...uh...he's taking a nap. What are you doing here?"

"Which way's his bedroom?" she asked, glancing around in dismay at the tiny, incredibly cluttered living room. Tissues, newspapers, toys, magazines, books, dirty socks, empty soda cans—Wade was a slob.

"It's...uh..." He looked for a moment as if he wasn't quite sure, and then he pointed. "That way."

"Lie down before you fall down. I'm going to look in on Clay, and then I'll be back to check on you."

"Emily..."

"Go lie down, Wade," she said a bit more sympathetically, watching as he swayed slightly on his bare feet. "I'll be right in."

She found Clay sound asleep in his bed, his *Star Wars* sheets rumpled around him, his stuffed tiger clasped in his arms. She brushed a lock of damp red hair away from his face, and laid her hand lightly on his cheek, satisfying herself that, while he was a bit warm, he wasn't dangerously feverish. He was sleeping so soundly that she thought he must have passed the worst of his illness and was now getting the rest he needed for full recuperation. Wade, however, was a different matter.

Emily smoothed Clay's sheets, then leaned over to brush a kiss on his soft cheek. How could she have ever imagined that taking care of this child would be a chore?

She would be back soon to wake him and encourage him to drink a glass of juice, but first she had to see about his father.

The bedroom to the left of Clay's was empty, the bed neatly made, nothing personal on the dresser or nightstand. Cecilia's recently vacated room, Emily suspected. Closing that door behind her, she crossed the hall.

Wade's room might have been large, and it might have been nicely furnished, but it was difficult to tell beneath the piles of sheets, clothes, more soda cans, tissues, more newspapers—compared to this room, the living room looked as though it had just had a good cleaning.

Wade lay facedown on the bed, groaning. "I'm going to die."

"You're not going to die." She knelt beside the bed, and stroked a damp strand of hair away from his face, much as she had with his son.

"I don't want you to get this."

"Don't worry about me. I've had a flu shot. That should help." She kissed his forehead, gauging his temperature with her lips. "You're burning up with fever."

"I'm disintegrating. Inch by inch."

"Wade...has anyone ever mentioned that you're a big baby when you're sick?"

"Maybe," he answered a bit sullenly.

"Hmm. I'm going to get you some juice and some aspirin. And then you can take a nap while I take a shovel to your living room."

"You haven't seen the kitchen yet," he muttered. "I haven't really felt like straightening up."

She winced, but stood up with renewed determination. "I'll be right back."

"Hurry. I don't want to die alone."

Emily was smiling ruefully as she left the room, pushing up the sleeves of her sweater in preparation for a long, busy afternoon.

SEVERAL HOURS LATER, after cooking soup and cleaning the house, cooling fevers and smoothing pillows, Emily collapsed onto Wade's sofa with a weary sigh. She was tired, but satisfied that both of the Davenport guys were on the road to recovery, though admittedly at different stages. Clay was much better. Wade most likely had a few miserable days of suffering still ahead of him.

She imagined that she looked a mess. She reached

for her purse, thinking that she would at least comb her hair and touch up her lipstick. Not that it mattered how she looked to Wade at the moment, she thought ruefully. But vanity won out.

Her purse, as always, was stuffed. She dug into it in search of a mirror and a lipstick. She pulled out a folded sheet of glossy paper and started to set it aside. And then something made her look at it more closely.

It was one of the travel brochures she'd been carrying around for so long. This one advertised an Alaskan cruise, and was decorated with photographs of glaciers and forests, sunsets over the ocean, sea creatures frolicking in the waves. She remembered gazing at this advertisement and imagining herself finding peace and contentment on the decks of a slow-moving cruise ship.

Now she knew that all she would find on that ship would be more of the loneliness and the longing for love that had haunted her in Honoria for most of her life.

Wade had told her that happiness wasn't a place, but a state of mind. She finally understood exactly what he had meant.

Just as she finally understood exactly what it was that made her happy.

TWENTY-FOUR HOURS later, Wade stumbled into his living room. Then he stopped, blinking at the transformation that had taken place since the last time he'd been in there. Everything was neatly put away. Fresh flowers had been arranged in the vase on the coffee table.

And on the couch, Emily and Clay were snuggled together while Emily read a Dr. Seuss story.

Wade felt as though a fist had hit him hard in the chest.

How was he going to say goodbye to her again?

Emily finished the story, then glanced up at the doorway where Wade stood. "Oh, hello. You must be feeling better. You're upright."

Embarrassed by how weak he'd been when she'd discovered him the day before, he squared his shoulders and tried to look hearty—though he wasn't sure how successful he was since he had to hold on to the doorjamb to keep himself from swaying. "Yeah, I'm better."

"Me, too," Clay piped up, his healthier coloring supporting his claim. "Miss Emily's been taking good care of me, Daddy."

Emily had been taking good care of both of them. First, she'd bullied Wade into staying in bed while she cleaned and cooked and served. Then she'd spent the night in Cecilia's former bedroom, getting up several times to check on Clay and to pump liquids and medicine into Wade. She'd brought him breakfast on a tray and hovered over him until she was satisfied that he'd eaten some of it.

He didn't know how she'd found out about the crisis in his household. He'd been determined not to call her. He hadn't wanted her to see him as just someone else who wanted to use her.

Holding his book, Clay scrambled off the couch. "I'm going to my room to watch TV. 'Beetleborgs' are coming on."

"Take a juice box with you," Emily called after him.

"You still need to drink plenty of liquids for a few days."

"Okay, Miss Emily." He dashed away, almost back to full speed.

Emily smiled at Wade again. "'Beetleborgs?'"

"Don't ask." Making a massive effort to look steady on his feet, Wade slowly crossed the room and lowered himself onto the other end of the couch.

Apparently, he hadn't fooled Emily for a minute. Frowning, she lifted a cool hand to his forehead. "You still have a fever," she announced. "Not as high as before, though."

"I sure hope you don't catch this. If I'd been thinking more clearly yesterday, I would have sent you straight home."

"You couldn't have made me leave," she returned firmly. "You and Clay needed me, Wade. Why didn't you call me?"

He didn't figure he really needed to answer that, considering the way they'd last parted. He leaned his aching head back against the couch, cursing himself for getting sick in the first place. This was not the way he wanted to be seen by the woman he loved. Why hadn't he taken the flu shot when he'd had the chance, instead of blithely assuming he was too tough to succumb to the virus?

"Wade?" Emily wasn't going to be satisfied with his silence. "Why *didn't* you call me?"

"I told you I wasn't looking for someone to take care of me and my son. That isn't what I want or what I need."

"I'm aware that you're perfectly capable of taking care of your family," Emily answered gently. "Even as sick as you were yesterday, you were taking good care of Clay. I could see that. But everyone needs help sometimes."

"And when they do, they usually call you. Isn't that what you've said?"

"And, as you pointed out, I've responded because I wanted to. I chose to be here with you and Clay this weekend, Wade. This is what I wanted to do. I don't expect you to apologize."

"Thanks."

She looked suddenly sheepish. "Have I really complained so much that you were reluctant to call me?"

"No. But you did mention that you've grown tired of taking care of others all the time."

She laced her fingers in her lap and gazed down at them. After a long, thoughtful moment, she sighed. "You know that my family life wasn't particularly happy, especially after my brother left town."

Wade nodded, thinking of all he'd heard about Emily's family...from her, and from others.

"My father's illness," she continued, "was long and horrible. It was as if he died an inch at a time. I couldn't have dealt with it twenty-four hours a day, so going to work every day was a relief for me. I was very fortunate that Dad's insurance provided full-time nursing during the days. But it was up to me to take care of him nights and weekends. You were right, of course. It was my choice to keep him at home, rather than putting him into a nursing facility. Dad and I were never close, but he was the only member of my immediate family who didn't actually abandon me. I owed him for that, if nothing else."

"You were a good daughter to him, Emily. He was the fortunate one."

"What really got me through these last few years was the fantasy of getting away. I spent hours studying travel guides, watching videos of places I wanted to visit, daydreaming of how wonderful it would be to be carefree and adventurous."

"And do you still think that's what you need to do to be happy? Travel and adventure?" he asked, knowing that he would have no choice but to stand aside and watch her go if she said yes. Hating the very thought of it.

"No," she whispered, giving him renewed hope.

"You're having second thoughts?"

She darted a quick glance at him, then looked back down at her hands. "Maybe."

"Any particular reason?" He almost held his breath as he waited for her answer.

"I think you know why," she murmured.

"I love you, Emily. I want to marry you and spend the rest of my life with you. But I don't want to talk you out of your dreams."

He had to say it, though what he really wanted to do was to take her in his arms and convince her once and for all that she never wanted to leave him.

"If you want to travel, I would love to travel with you. We'll spend our vacations exploring together. But if you need to go without me—if you need to travel and be alone for a while to think about what you want—I'll wait. And if you decide that I'm not what you want, what you need—well, I'll survive."

Somehow.

She searched his face with anxious eyes. "Wade, are

you really sure? I mean, you really haven't known me very long, and I haven't been at my best most of the time...how can you know?"

Her suddenly urgent tone took him aback for a moment. He frowned, tilting his head to look at her more closely. "Are you asking if I'm sure that I love you?"

She nodded, biting her lower lip until he was concerned she was going to make it bleed.

He laid his hand over hers, feeling the tension in her tightly locked fingers. "I thought I'd already made myself clear on this. I love you. I have from the start, I think. It has nothing to do with what you can do for me, and everything to do with who you are."

He was suddenly struck by a realization that made him feel like smacking his forehead and saying, "Aha!" A significant piece of the puzzle that was Emily had just fallen into place in his mind.

"It's very hard for you to believe that someone could love you just for yourself, isn't it, sweetheart?" he asked gently, holding her hands in both of his. "Everyone you loved left you...your father emotionally, the others physically. And maybe their defection made you wonder if there was something lacking in you. Something you had to make up for by being more perfect, more helpful, more accommodating than anyone else."

She frowned. "Since when are you a psychoanalyst?"

"No, I'm not a psychoanalyst. Just a man in love with a woman he wants very badly to understand."

"And you think you understand me now?"

"I don't know. Do I?"

She looked at him for a long time, her eyes shuttered. And then she smiled wryly. "Maybe."

"I don't want you to ever doubt that you're worthy of love, Emily. Your family had problems, but they had nothing to do with you. Nothing you did sent them away. They left because they needed to, for reasons of their own. And if you leave...then it should be because you want to, not because you're afraid to stay."

This time she didn't say anything as she continued to look at him.

Wade drew a deep breath, then took the final gamble. "I want you to be happy. I'd like to spend the rest of my life keeping you that way, if you'll let me. If you want to see the world, I'll go with you. If you want to see it alone, I'll wait for you here. I love you. I won't ever stop loving you."

Her blue eyes were suddenly so bright, so vivid that it took his breath away. "All my life," she whispered, "I've been working to make people love me. But whatever I did, it never seemed to be enough. You're the first one to ask what would make *me* happy."

"And do you know what that is?" he asked a bit hoarsely.

"I'm beginning to." She smiled crookedly. "You were wrong about one thing, you know. I wasn't leaving to run away from anything. I was leaving to find something."

"And that was...?"

"Excitement. Adventure. Love. A purpose for my life. I never thought I could find those things here, in Honoria. I never expected that they would come to me." She turned her hands over to clasp his. "I never expected you, Wade Davenport."

He lifted her hands to his lips. "I love you, Emily."

"I was so afraid to believe that. So afraid that I would mess it up, somehow. Afraid that I couldn't work hard enough, or be perfect enough to make you keep loving me. But you know I'm not perfect, don't you, Wade? You know my fears and my flaws and the baggage I carry. And you love me, anyway."

"Yes. And you know I'm far from perfect. That I've got flaws and fears and baggage of my own."

"And I love you, anyway," she whispered.

It was the first time she'd said it. He closed his eyes in reaction, feeling the relief flood through him. His head was beginning to swim again, either from flu or emotion, or a combination of both.

"I'm too weak to drag this out much longer," he murmured. "Are you trying to tell me that you're going to stay?"

"I'm telling you that there's no longer any reason for me to go. I've found everything I ever wanted right here with you," she answered simply. Sincerely. "I love you, Wade. I love your son. I want to be a family with you, to give you both all the love I've been saving inside me for so long. I want to live in a house that's so full of love and laughter and joy that it almost bursts at the seams."

"You'll never have to doubt that I love you," he promised. "Even when I'm irked with you...and that's going to happen, Emily. I'm afraid it's impossible for two people to live together without teeing each other off occasionally."

She laughed suddenly, musically, and his chest clenched. "I know. I'll get mad at you, too. In fact, I was furious with you yesterday because I had to hear from

Martha Godwin that you and Clay were sick. But I still loved you."

He winced. "Martha Godwin?"

She nodded. "I'll tell you about it later. Promise me, Wade, that you'll always feel free to tell me what you need from me."

"Promise me that you'll always feel free to say no. That you won't feel you have to earn my love. And that you'll never hesitate to ask for what *you* need."

"I need something right now," she said, the satisfyingly happy glitter still bright in her eyes.

"Anything," he vowed recklessly.

"Take your medicine and go lie down. I want you well, and soon, so I can take advantage of you without worrying about killing you."

This time it was Wade who laughed, and then groaned with frustration. "Oh, man. This is a really lousy time to have the flu."

"Next year, maybe you'll get your flu shot," she said primly. "Go to bed, Wade."

He sighed deeply as he stood, half-seriously hoping he wasn't delirious and imagining all this. "You'll be here when I wake up?"

She stood with him, and wrapped her arms around him for a fervent hug. "I'll be here for as long as you want me," she whispered.

He lifted her off her feet and held her tightly, proving to both of them that his illness hadn't totally weakened him. "Forever. I'll want you forever."

"Then you're in luck," she whispered. "That's exactly how long I was planning to stay."

Epilogue

"IT WAS a beautiful wedding, wasn't it?"

Wade snuggled Emily more tightly against his bare body and gave a typically male answer to such a question. "Mmm."

"Tara looked so beautiful. And Blake so handsome. And Savannah and the twins looked so happy with Kit."

"Mmm." Wade seemed much more interested in re-exploring Emily's curves than in recapping the wedding they'd attended several hours earlier.

Emily giggled and caught his hand when it wandered dangerously close to trouble—again. "It's only been a few days since you were down with the flu. Are you sure you want to risk a relapse?"

"Woman, are you questioning my stamina?" he asked, sounding properly indignant.

"Never," she promised with mock gravity.

"I'm glad you talked me into coming to the wedding with you," he said, shifting their positions to give him access to her throat, which he then proceeded to nuzzle.

She smiled, sliding her fingers into his hair. The gold bracelet on her wrist glinted in the lamplight as her arm moved. The bracelet had been a gift from Wade, its heart-shaped links representing his love for her. When he'd given it to her two days ago, he had told her with touching uncertainty that he knew it couldn't replace the one that had been her mother's. He had promised not to stop looking for her mother's bracelet, though he'd admitted that the chances of recovery grew slimmer with each day it was missing.

With tears in her eyes, Emily had assured him that this bracelet meant even more to her. It had been bought with love, for her alone. And given to her by someone who would never retract that love, who would never abandon her.

She hadn't taken the bracelet off since he'd clasped it around her wrist.

She hadn't had to work very hard to convince Wade to accompany her to Tara's wedding on this Friday after Thanksgiving. Leaving Clay to spend the night with the family of his best friend from school, Wade and Emily had slipped away for one night together in a lovely Atlanta hotel following her cousin's wedding. They had to return to Honoria early the next day, but they intended to make good use of these rare hours together.

Wade kissed her lingeringly, pressing her into the well-rumpled sheets. "I love you," he murmured.

She arched into his weight. "I love you, too."

"I want to spend every night with you like this." Tangling his legs with hers, he teased her with playful thrusts of his body, until her smile faded and she was aching with renewed desire. "I want to wake every morning with you in my arms."

"I want that, too," she whispered, pulling him closer.

He slipped inside her with an ease that only proved

they were made for each other. "Marry me soon, Emily. Tomorrow. Now."

"We'll be a family by Christmas," she promised. "Now do me a favor, Chief. Be quiet and kiss me."

"All you had to do was ask," he answered with a flash of smile. And then he kissed her until she was no longer capable of coherent speech.

He spent the rest of the night giving her everything she had ever wanted. He took her places she'd never been. Gave her experiences she'd only fantasized about before. And filled her heart with so much love that she knew it would never be empty again.

Wait! The story's not over yet....
The prodigal son is about to return.
Lucas McBride, Emily's long-lost brother is coming
home for Christmas...and to settle the score.
Don't miss the fireworks!
Available in December, wherever Harlequin books
are sold.

HARLEQUIN® *Temptation*

*It's a dating wasteland out there! So what's
a girl to do when there's not a marriage-
minded man in sight? Go hunting, of course.*

Manhunting

Enjoy the hilarious antics of five intrepid heroines,
determined to lead Mr. Right to the altar—
whether he wants to go or not!

She's got a plan—to find herself a man!

Available wherever Harlequin books are sold.

Take 2 bestselling love stories FREE
Plus get a FREE surprise gift!

Special Limited-Time Offer

Mail to Harlequin Reader Service®

3010 Walden Avenue
P.O. Box 1867
Buffalo, N.Y. 14240-1867

YES! Please send me 2 free Harlequin Temptation® novels and my free surprise gift. Then send me 4 brand-new novels every month, which I will receive before they appear in bookstores. Bill me at the low price of $3.12 each plus 25¢ delivery and applicable sales tax, if any.* That's the complete price, and a saving of over 10% off the cover prices—quite a bargain! I understand that accepting the books and gift places me under no obligation ever to buy any books. I can always return a shipment and cancel at any time. Even if I never buy another book from Harlequin, the 2 free books and the surprise gift are mine to keep forever.

142 HEN CH7G

Name	(PLEASE PRINT)	
Address	Apt. No.	
City	State	Zip

This offer is limited to one order per household and not valid to present Harlequin Temptation® subscribers. *Terms and prices are subject to change without notice. Sales tax applicable in N.Y.

UTEMP-98   ©1990 Harlequin Enterprises Limited

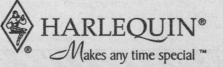

It's hot...
and it's out of control!

This summer, Temptation turns up the heat.
Look for these bold, provocative,
***ultra*-sexy books!**

#686 *SEDUCING SULLIVAN*
Julie Elizabeth Leto
June 1998

Angela Harris had only one obsession—Jack Sullivan.
Ever since high school, he'd been on her mind...and
in her fantasies. But no more. At her ten-year
reunion, she was going to get him out of her system
for good. All she needed was one sizzling night with
Jack—and then she could get on with her life.
Unfortunately she hadn't counted on Jack having a
few obsessions of his own....

BLAZE! Red-hot reads from

HARLEQUIN®

Temptation

DEBBIE MACOMBER

invites you to the

HEART OF TEXAS

Join Debbie Macomber as she brings you the lives and loves of the folks in the ranching community of Promise, Texas.

If you loved Midnight Sons—don't miss Heart of Texas! A brand-new six-book series from Debbie Macomber.

Available in February 1998 at your favorite retail store.

Heart of Texas by Debbie Macomber

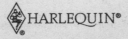

HARLEQUIN®

HPHRT1

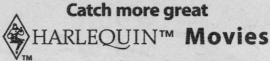

COMING NEXT MONTH

#685 MANHUNTING IN MISSISSIPPI Stephanie Bond
Manhunting...

Piper Shepherd, the only single member of her sorority, was going
to find a husband—or else. But the pickin's *were* pretty slim in
Mudville, Mississippi, population twenty! Then a gorgeous
stranger arrived in town. Piper thought she'd found Mr. Right—
until she noticed his ring....

#686 SEDUCING SULLIVAN Julie Elizabeth Leto
Blaze

Angela Harris had only one obsession—Jack Sullivan. Ever since
high school he'd been on her mind...and in her fantasies. But no
more. At her ten-year reunion, she was going to get him out of her
system for good! One steamy night with Jack—and then she could
get on with her life. Unfortunately, she hadn't counted on Jack
having a few obsessions of his own....

#687 DREAMS Rita Clay Estrada

Greg Torrance was a dream come true for Mary Ellen Gallagher.
Not only was he tall, dark *and* handsome, but he offered her big
money for the work she loved to do! The nightmare began when
she fell in love with her sexy client—only to discover his heart
belonged to someone else...whether he knew it or not.

#688 A DIAMOND IN THE ROUGH Selina Sinclair
Sara Matthews had to find an impressive date for the party where
her ex-fiancé would announce his engagement to another woman.
Dark, mysterious Dakota Wilder was *perfect*. Dakota hated parties,
but he did fancy Sara, so they struck an outrageous deal. He'd
find her a date...if she let him seduce her!

AVAILABLE NOW:

#681 MANHUNTING IN MIAMI
Alyssa Dean

#682 PRIVATE FANTASIES
Janelle Denison

#683 HUNK OF THE MONTH
JoAnn Ross

#684 ENTICING EMILY
Gina Wilkins